HIS AMIABLE BRIDE

ALSO BY KASEY STOCKTON

Women of Worth Series

Love in the Bargain

Love for the Spinster

Love at the House Party

Love in the Wager

Love in the Ballroom

Ladies of Devon Series

The Jewels of Halstead Manor

Stand-alone Historical Romance

A Duke for Lady Eve, Belles of Christmas

A Forgiving Heart, Seasons of Change Series

Contemporary Romance

Snowflake Wishes

His Stand-In Holiday Girlfriend

Snowed In on Main Street

HIS *Amiable* BRIDE

KASEY STOCKTON

GOLDEN  OWL
PRESS

For those who give selflessly; the purest form of love.

CHAPTER 1

$\mathcal{C}$oriander Miranda Featherbottom held a breath of air hostage in her lungs while her fingers curled tightly around each other in her lap. She counted to ten; then she counted backward. The focus it took to hold her breath muted her mother's high-pitched droning into a softer whine. She absently watched her mother's mouth moving until tiny black spots pricked her outer vision and she released the captive air, resuming her breathing and regaining a sense of composure.

That was close. Next time she'd need to be sure not to hold her breath quite so long. It would never do to faint with company present.

Quiet fell over the room and Cori glanced at her mother's eyes which were now locked on her. She sat up straighter—if that was even possible—and watched her mother's head cock slightly to the side as her eyebrows went up expectantly. Oh, no. They'd asked her a question.

"I am sorry, Mama, I wasn't attending," Cori said softly, delivering a smile she hoped was apologetic.

"Quite so," Rosemary muttered from the chair beside her.

Cori stifled the urge to kick her sister's shin and broadened her smile until her cheeks grew sore.

"I was only just mentioning to Lady Berwind here that you would be perfectly happy to visit Windfall's dower house on Monday next and ensure her mother-in-law is settled."

Cori refrained from glancing at her older sister as she said, "Indeed, ma'am. I should be delighted."

"That is settled, then." Lady Berwind hefted herself up, heedless of the small dog settled on her lap. He woke and landed on his tiny feet in one motion, obediently remaining near his mistress. "It sets my mind at ease to know my dear mama-in-law shall be watched over in my absence."

Cori suppressed a snort and smiled at the regal marchioness while her mother and sister bid her farewell and a safe journey to Town. She was more likely seething that her mama-in-law should deign to move into the dower house after vulgarly living abroad and was conveniently making her own self scarce to avoid the ghastly woman.

The room remained quiet as they listened to Lady Berwind's carriage door close, followed by the clip-clop of the horses hooves as they removed her from the Featherbottom's drive. When she was finally gone, they let out a collective sigh.

"I should think," Cori ventured cautiously, "perhaps Rose would have been better suited for the task. It is she that hopes to join their family, after all."

"Quite so," Mama answered; her gaze swung from Cori's plain face to that of her radiant sister. "But Rose will be better equipped to secure Lord Arnett in the drawing rooms of London. No need to leave her here, cozying up to the man's grandmama."

"What? You're to go to London?" Cori protested, though she hardly knew why she bothered. It would only be natural for her mother to take her older sister to London and leave her quite alone at home again.

"Cori," Mama said in exasperation, "Shall you never listen? I was just mentioning to the marchioness that we leave for London on the morrow. Mourning has quite delayed Rosemary's return to society long enough, I should think, and it is time to reintroduce her to the *ton*."

"But what about me?" Cori winced at the whine in her voice, but Lady Berwind was gone, and therefore her composure need not be absolutely perfect.

"You will have your turn," Mama said, standing, "after Rose is married to Lord Arnett." She gave Rosemary a telling look. "Once Rose secures her place in the Arnett family, then doors will open to you that otherwise would be unobtainable. Just remain patient."

Rosemary stood and gracefully followed her mother from the room, tossing a careless look over her shoulder. Cori listened to their conversation drift away, discussing which gowns to have packed and what they should venture to purchase on arrival in Town. She sank further in her chair, abandoning her ladylike composure.

Drat her distraction! If only she had listened earlier to Lady Berwind, she would have heard exactly what had happened. Lady Berwind must have announced a plan to retire to London for the Season, prompting Cori's own mother to mimic the plan. If history were any indication, both women pretended they'd had just such a decision in mind all along. And perhaps Lady Berwind did—she'd likely planned her departure as soon as she heard her mother-in-law was set to take up residence. But Cori's mother and Rosemary were still weeks away from their originally scheduled departure.

Cori huffed. To follow Lady Berwind to London just so Rosemary could ensnare her son, and the future Marquess, Lord Arnett, felt ridiculous. But then, maybe Cori would feel differently if she wasn't being left behind.

Mmmmm. Cori let out a delicious sigh. *Lord Arnett.*

Undoubtedly the most handsome man she had ever met. The red-headed earl was a tall man with kind eyes and had been Cori's closest neighbor for all of her life. Close in proximity, but remote in every other regard. His younger brother, Lord Travis, had been her tree climbing companion for many of her younger years, but since he'd set off for school at the age of twelve, she rarely saw him.

Once when Cori was eleven or so, Lord Arnett had come upon her and Travis in the woods behind Windfall, the Arnett family home. Travis had been showing off, swinging from a low branch, certainly not high enough for any major injury should he fall. Still, when he tumbled to the ground, Lord Arnett had run to his brother's side, shouting at Cori to retrieve help at once. She'd obeyed, the command impossible to refuse, but not before catching fear and concern lace the features of Lord Arnett as he looked over his younger brother's swollen ankle. His consideration had struck a chord within Cori then, and developed into an admiration that filled her young, inexperienced heart.

Lord Arnett must have returned from his time abroad in Italy to spend the Season in London, or so Cori assumed. Otherwise, Mama surely would not find it necessary to grace London with her own presence. With five children to care for—four of whom had the audacity to be girls and thus required marrying off—Mama did not take herself off to London for any small reason.

Cori stood and stretched out her weary arms, considering her situation. Perhaps it would've been different had she been born a beauty like her sister. She'd done all she could to remain out of the sun, but some freckles did not require sunlight to appear. Her nose was straight and nondescript, her face oval. She was neither thin nor plump; not tall and certainly not short. Coriander Featherbottom was unremarkably ordinary.

She did, however, possess two distinct features she secretly hoped balanced the scales a smidge in her own favor. Her eyebrows held a sleek, dark arch that perfectly framed her eyes, and her eyelashes were naturally long and curly. They had the appearance of being darkened with kohl without actually needing to use the cosmetic. She was not delusional, however, and knew that obtaining a husband would be infinitely easier once her tall, elegant sister married Lord Arnett, and Cori's social status rose accordingly. Her own dowry was just like everything else in her life and person, it was also quite average.

She listened to the thumping and banging of rushed packing taking place upstairs while Mama and Rosemary prepared for their trip. Papa, no doubt, would be taken along to Town, for he was quite in love with his overbearing wife and oddly wished to be with her nearly always. As focused as he was on Mrs. Featherbottom's happiness, Mrs. Featherbottom reserved her attentions for their children—or, more accurately, on securing their children's place in the world.

Cori grumbled. She understood *why* she should be left behind. She was rather useless when it came to husband hunting. But that did not make it any easier to bear. Still, someone did need to stay and watch over her youngest two sisters. The gap being rather large between Basil, Cori's younger brother, and Meg and Marjie, it often fell to Cori to see to the girl's needs when their mother was absent from home.

Determined to think no more on the matter, Cori escaped to the stables and her mare, Chance. She wasn't dressed for riding, but she hardly cared. After a stable hand readied Chance, she took off, urging her horse into a gallop the moment they hit the open fields. The wind streaming in her hair and the feel of bunched muscles beneath her were as familiar as her own skin, and Cori breathed as one with Chance; for a moment it felt as though they even outran her insecurities.

Her mind conjured up the last glimpse she'd had of Lord Arnett when he took leave of her father a year prior, before setting off for Italy. She had watched from the upper gallery in her home while he spoke to Mr. Featherbottom about some gentlemanly pursuit. He had rubbed the back of his neck continually, as though plagued with anxiety or unease or some such feeling, and she'd longed to go down and soothe him, to discover the cause of his edginess. Instead, she'd watched Rosemary approach him; he had visibly stiffened, taking his leave shortly after their brief conversation. What Cori still did not understand was the intense look in his eye when he'd said farewell to Rose.

Kicking her heel into the side of her brown mare, Cori leaned forward, urging her horse toward a row of hedges. Taking the jump in stride, she soaked in the feeling of flying. There was one place she did not compete and lose against her older, perfect sister: on horseback. Perhaps that was why she loved it so.

Turning Chance around, she caught another hedge in her peripheral. Papa said it was too high, but nevermind that. He was simply being cautious. He just didn't have enough faith in her.

No one did.

Fire started in Cori's breast and burned until she turned Chance. Gaining speed, she approached the hedge quickly. Faster, in fact, than she had anticipated. At the last second, she balked. Pulling up on Chance's reigns with all of the strength she possessed, she turned the horse and continued to gallop alongside the row of hedges.

Her body filled with anger; at her father for doubting her, but more for doubting herself. She rode Chance long and hard until the anger dissipated into a faint irritation. It was not until they returned to the stables that she noticed her horse gleaming with sweat and panting. Immediate regret touched her heart and she walked Chance into her stall herself after the sidesaddle was removed. She brushed the mare and fed her a bag of oats, murmuring words of apology as she soothed the overworked beast.

The sun was low in the sky by the time she returned home and dressed for dinner. She made it through the meal listening to Mama and Rosemary discuss their last-minute preparations for travel. She swallowed the indignation she felt whenever one of them mentioned London.

She reminded herself that when Rosemary married Lord Arnett, it would benefit Cori. She would have to get over her childhood infatuation if she was ever to accept Lord Arnett as a brother. But she would, eventually. It was only a small tendre, after all.

The following morning, she stood at the window and watched the carriage drive away carrying Rosemary and her parents. They planned on surprising her brother, Basil, at the London townhouse; Cori did not envy that reunion. He would be furious to be so set upon, but no one foresaw as much except her. She thought about trying to warn her family, but there was no point. None of them would have listened anyway.

A slow sigh escaped Cori's lips, tension leaving her shoulders. There was one benefit to being left behind: freedom.

Cori turned away from the window and climbed the stairs to the schoolroom. Maybe Meg and Marjie would want to spend the morning outside.

CHAPTER 2

"*T*he post, Miss Cori." Harvey held out a silver platter with a single sealed missive resting in its center. Cori retrieved the letter and thanked the butler before slicing open the waxed seal with her penknife and unfolding the creased paper. She skimmed the note before relaying its finer points to her sister, Meg.

"Basil is none too pleased at being 'ambushed,' as he says it."

Meg smiled. "I do not understand our brother. Shouldn't he be happy to receive Mama and Papa? He's living in their townhouse, after all." At thirteen, Meg could be profoundly wise at times.

"But we know Basil, don't we? They've never gotten on."

Meg sighed. "When shall we expect him?"

Cori looked sharply at her sister. Just as she thought—quite wise indeed. "Within a few days, I imagine."

Meg nodded before returning to her book.

"He doesn't own as much in his letter," Cori continued, "but I'm sure he is coming out of spite. He hardly graces us with his presence the whole year round, but when Mama expects his help squiring Rose about Town, he's suddenly yearning for his country home? Too convenient, if you ask me."

"Perhaps it is just as well no one has asked you," Meg said into her book. Cori shot her a wry smile and took a moment to watch her little sister. Though opposite in every other regard, Meg was growing more like Rosemary in appearance every day. Both Meg and Marjie shared Rosemary's fair hair and porcelain complexion, and the three of them laid claim to clear blue eyes that matched Basil's exactly. The younger girls had yet to grow into their own completely, but it was apparent they would take after Basil and Rosemary in their tall willowy frames, too.

If not for the direct likeness Cori shared with her mother, she would believe herself adopted.

"Do you think Rosemary will have any luck with Lord Arnett?"

Cori whipped her head around so quickly she heard a slight pop. "Pardon me?"

Meg was still looking down at her book, a small smile gracing her lips. "After what she did to him, I would be quite shocked to hear of an immediate betrothal."

"I cannot understand you, sister. Rosemary could have any man she chooses. She'll have her pick just like she did the first time around."

"If you are talking about her betrothal to Lord Hammond, then so am I."

"You are speaking in riddles," Cori said, suddenly annoyed. "It is only you and I in this room, I beg you will speak plainly. What have you overheard?"

Meg closed her book and looked up at her sister with deliberate care. "Rose trailed many suitors along after her first season, and even more after her second. I have overheard nothing particular, but I believe Lord Arnett thought himself quite above the rest when she shocked us all and accepted Lord Hammond's suit."

"I do not believe it was quite that big of a shock, Meg. Hammond was a duke."

Was. The man died not three months into their betrothal, leaving Rose to go into mourning and throwing her back into the market, so to speak, without even the benefit of his title.

Meg said, "Perhaps Lord Arnett was in love with Rose, and thought she returned the sentiment."

Cori ruminated over this. No doubt Lord Arnett had been in love with Rosemary. He was not only among her more ardent admirers, but he took himself off to the continent only a few weeks after her announced betrothal to the duke, and remained there for just over a year. Surely he had been mending a broken heart. But now he was back in London, and Rosemary as well, with the late Lord Hammond decidedly out of the picture. A betrothal between them was imminent. It *had* to be.

"Shall we place a wager?" Meg asked with uncharacteristic glee. "I can see you doubt me. I shall bet you your jonquil evening gown that Arnett does not offer for Rose."

"How very unladylike, Meg," Cori said, feigning disbelief. She smiled slowly and added, "I accept."

BASIL ARRIVED THAT EVENING, shocking his sisters by both his swiftness and his audacity; he arrived with not one friend in tow, but three.

"A hunting party?" Cori tried to keep her voice calm. Basil had deposited his friends in the drawing room before seeking her out for a private word.

His grin was sheepish. "It is my home too, Cori. Besides, they aren't staying here. They'll sleep at the inn."

She tried to slow her growing irritation. "You will be dining with them at the inn, as well? They cannot be here, Basil. Mama would not abide it."

"I will, in future," he said, unrepentant. "I've already promised them a meal tonight."

"Then I shall dine upstairs with Meg and Marjie." Cori spun to leave and threw a parting shot. "I hope you've at least warned cook about the extra bellies she is to fill."

She imagined the look of chagrin which should have crossed Basil's face, but knowing her brother as she did, she rather assumed he shrugged off her disdain and went into dinner without a care in the world. It would be improper for her to dine with single men, regardless of Basil's presence. But of course, he would not think of that, for she was ineligible. To be eligible, one had to be considered in the first place. The only thing Cori was considered for was how she could be of service to those around her.

Suppressing her irritation, she enjoyed dinner beside her younger sisters. Meg was quiet and thoughtful, sprinkling her carefully thought out opinions amidst the chaos which embodied Marjie. At nine years old, Marjie was still quite the handful. She had an overabundance of energy and enthusiasm for life that balanced Meg's quiet restfulness.

"Tomorrow will you take us to the creek? I should like to take my new puppy to splash in the water. Dogs like water. I heard it from Billy."

"The stable hand?" Meg inquired.

"Of course. There's no other Billy," Marjie scoffed.

"If you complete your lessons, I would be happy to walk to the creek with you," Cori said "But you must understand, Basil has brought friends from London and they intend to hunt. We must make sure the way is clear and safe before we venture out."

Marjie grinned and jumped onto Cori's lap. "At nine, my dear, I believe you are past the age of sitting in my lap," Cori said with a laugh.

Marjie gave her a look which could only be described as

impish, throwing her arms around her sister's neck and squeezing. "I just love you so, Cori." She finished off the brown nosing with a kiss on the cheek and jumped to her feet before skipping to the playroom next door.

"She knows precisely how adorable she is," Meg said without lifting her nose from her book.

"And you don't?" Cori countered, thinking of how easily Meg could twist their father around her little finger. Meg only smiled, her eyes never leaving her page.

CHAPTER 3

The following morning dawned beautiful, promising a clear, sunny day. Cori woke Basil to inform him of her creek plans, assuring their safety from hunters, at least for the morning.

The sisters retrieved Marjie's new puppy from the kitchen where she was currently being house trained and fashioned a leash around her neck before making their way outside. The crisp, cool air lifted her spirits and etched a smile onto Cori's face she felt sure would remain there the rest of the day.

The spaniel, Annabelle, proved Billy's decree and played joyously in the shallow water, bringing delight to Marjie as well as her more refined sisters. They took turns throwing a stick and directing Annabelle to retrieve it.

"I think I should like to bring my watercolors to this very spot," Cori said reflectively. The light was shining on the water, sparkling against the wet rocks. The bank rose gradually, blanketed with grass and dotted with crisp leaves. The opposite side of the creek was a deep wood underneath a clear, cloudless sky. She would most likely add a few puffy white clouds for effect, but otherwise, the scene was perfect.

Cori had just imagined the perfect color combination to get the sky just the right shade of blue when she was suddenly ambushed. Annabelle jumped on her, knocking the air from her lungs as paws planted her down by her shoulders. Decidedly foul breath washed over her face while a rough tongue licked up the side of her neck, causing her to shriek with giggles. The dog must have taken the laughter as a good sign, for she did not cease her ministrations. Meg and Marjie ran to Cori's aid but fell over themselves with unrestrained laughter.

Cori managed one loud shriek of, "Help me!" before succumbing to another bout of hysterical laughter, but her younger sisters made no move to call Annabelle off.

A thunderous sound rumbled beneath her body and Annabelle jumped off of Cori, taking a protective stance over her torso instead. She tilted her head back to watch the approaching rider and her heart sped when she caught the shock of red hair beneath the gentleman's hat. But no, it could not be Lord Arnett. Surely it was only his brother. Struggling to catch her breath, she turned back to Meg. "Call her off!"

Meg obliged and Annabelle was soon distracted with another throwing stick. Cori shook her head at the short attention span of the puppy only to see ratty strands of her dark hair falling forward on her face. She groaned slightly, hearing the rider jump down from his horse. Shaking the last few pins out of her hair, she scraped it back behind her head and out of her face before turning back to Lord Travis.

"My lord, you must forgive my appearance—"

Cori sucked in a breath as she came face to face with a redheaded man who was quite clearly changed—and most certainly not Lord Travis. The sun had warmed his skin, adding a mass amount of freckles; somehow they made his hair look all the brighter. His hard, green eyes looked questioningly into hers and she realized he must have wondered who she was, and how she knew him.

"Yes?" he inquired.

She curtseyed. "I am Miss Cori Featherbottom. I apologize, I almost mistook you for your brother."

A smile played at his lips. "Alas, I could never mistake you for your sister."

She felt umbrage at that remark. Was he implying a competition between the sisters? If it was, she failed. And it was ungentlemanly of him, to say the least.

"No, do not set up your back at me," he continued. "Believe it or not, I intended that as a compliment."

He had to be teasing, surely. "Is there any way I can be of service?" Cori asked stiffly. She found her previous hero worship of the enticingly dashing gentleman quickly dissipating. Nothing quite set her off like a reminder of how very far she fell below Rosemary in every regard.

"I had rather thought I was going to be offering the service." He gave her a slow perusal which naturally straightened her spine. "From a distance, it looked as though you were being devoured by wild beasts."

She gave a pointed look at Annabelle laying beside Marjie, her pink tongue lolling on the grass as she caught her breath.

"Well, your screams were frightening," Lord Arnett defended, taking note of the large puppy, an auburn eyebrow raised.

"I apologize for the confusion. I was being...tickled." Heat rushed up her neck at the remark.

"Ah. Noted. I'll be sure to avoid the practice in future." he said under his breath.

The heat pulsing in her cheeks flared into a fiery hot flame. "Come along, girls. We must be heading back." Cori turned away without formally taking her leave. She had not known Lord Arnett very well before he left for Italy; she'd simply admired him from afar. It would appear that looks could be deceiving. Either that or Italy had changed the man thoroughly.

He was rude and inappropriate. Earl or not, she would not allow anyone to speak to her in such a way.

"No, no, not like this." Lord Arnett stopped her with a hand on her elbow. She looked pointedly at it until he released her and she turned to face him.

"Let me try again," he said. "You owe me, really. I truly thought you were being ruthlessly attacked."

In retrospect, she could see that possibility. She stared into Lord Arnett's clear green eyes a beat too long—it was truly easy to become lost in them—then shook herself back into the moment. "Thank you for trying to rescue me," she conceded.

Lord Arnett delivered a magnetic smile. Rosemary was quite lucky, indeed.

"We really should be getting home," Cori repeated. She turned and gave her sisters meaningful looks and they hurried to her side.

"Then allow me to escort you," Lord Arnett said.

Giving him a curious eye, Cori nodded and they all started toward the Featherbottom estate.

"Are you recently returned home, my lord?" Cori asked by way of making conversation. What she truly wanted to know was if he had already proposed to Rosemary. If the man was going to become her brother, she ought to try and see him in that light.

"Only last night, actually. I have been in London for some time and traveling the continent before that."

Cori nodded. It would not do to admit that she had followed his travels closely. He might look at her little tendre as something of a nuisance.

"My parents are in Town at present," Cori ventured carefully. "They took my sister for the Season."

Lord Arnett nodded but said nothing. He walked beside her, his hands clasped behind his back while he led his magnificent chestnut horse. Marjie and Meg walked ahead of them with Annabelle reattached to her leash.

"You do not join them in Town?" he asked at length.

"No," she responded some moments later, offering no further explanation.

"Do you visit with Eleanor at all? She attended the season just this past year, I believe." He must have been searching for a topic.

Cori tried not to stiffen her posture, but it was in vain. "Lady Eleanor and I are of very little acquaintance, sir. She is quite a few years younger than I am." Cori did not mention she had yet to attend any season herself, despite her aging years.

Stilted silence resumed between them.

Something stirred within Cori. The silence wouldn't do.

In a way, the walk was a dream come true. After so many days of watching and admiring Lord Arnett from a distance, Cori finally had the opportunity to converse with him. She could not allow the opportunity to go wasted, turning into some meaningless encounter Lord Arnett would surely forget. Soaking in the privilege he currently offered her, she threw caution to the wind.

"Did you enjoy the continent?"

"Very much, although..." he trailed off, looking away.

"Yes?"

He glanced at her, smiling slightly. "It was not home."

What an odd thing to say. "No, I can imagine it was not."

Silence overcame them once more. It was more comfortable, but also disappointing. Why could she not just *speak*?

"Are you all right?" he asked.

"Of course," Cori said quickly. "Why do you ask?"

"You appear as if you have sucked on a lemon."

"Thank you, sir," she said dryly. "I shall keep that in mind."

"Been thinking about something distasteful?" he pried.

"Perhaps." She tried to sound mysterious. Though this older, experienced man could likely see right through her.

Lord Arnett let out a booming laugh. All right, perhaps she only sounded ridiculous.

It was with great relief that her home came into view. Basil and his friends were in front of the stables, retrieving guns from servants and climbing onto horses.

Lord Arnett stopped short and Cori was startled to find his face turned to stone. "My brother has brought friends home for a hunting party," she supplied.

"And your family?"

"My sisters and I do not hunt, sir."

He tore his gaze from the group of riders and settled on her face. She felt utterly stripped. "Your parents?"

"Remain in London," she answered.

He nodded once before picking up her hand and kissing the back of it. Her breath caught at the romantic gesture and her heart sped. "I must be off," he said, swinging onto his horse. "Good day, Miss Featherbottom."

Cori watched him ride away, back in the direction of his own land. He did not even approach the house to greet Basil. What strange behavior.

She turned and followed her sisters upstairs to change out of her muddy, dog-stomped dress. Meg and Marjie returned to the schoolroom, and Cori ordered herself a bath. Not only did she look horrid, but she smelled like wet dog. What an absolutely perfect way to spend her time with Lord Arnett.

ADAM ARNETT RODE HARD. Logically, he realized *she* was not at home, but seeing Basil and his cronies had done something to his equilibrium and he found himself needing the exercise.

It wasn't enough that Travis was avoiding him, but now Rosemary followed his family to London, showing up at his house with her doe eyes and false innocence. Could she not retract her claws and leave him to make his own choice?

Frustrated, Adam took the long way back to Windfall. The sight of the Featherbottom girl being mauled slipped into his thoughts. Her scream had set something off in his blood and he rushed to get to her. It wasn't until he got closer that he had seen her laughter and that of her sisters—an immediate war of relief and irritation swarming within him. It was his intention to leave them be, but he found himself drawn to the girl. Her directness, perhaps?

Plainly, she was unlike Rosemary.

Jumping a hedge, Adam shook frustration from his shoulders. He was going to ride out the irritation all day if he had to, but one way or another he was going to find a way to get his mother and Rosemary to leave him be once and for all.

CHAPTER 4

$\mathcal{C}$ ori went for many walks after running into Lord
Arnett, nearly every day the weather allowed, but did
not run into him again. It was a pity, for she had taken great care
in her dress and appearance before each lengthy ramble, and all
for nothing. What was the point of looking her best if she
wasn't even going to see anyone worthwhile?

When the Dowager Lady Berwind arrived at Windfall's
dower house with a fine equipage loaded to the brim with
souvenirs of her many travels, Cori promptly visited, as she
promised she would. At least the dowager might appreciate her
attempts to elevate her dress and appearance. The Dowager
welcomed her graciously, and invited her back again to help
with the sorting and arranging of her many decorative
possessions.

Cori left the dower house completely baffled by Lady
Berwind's outward disdain for her mother-in-law. How anyone
could dislike such a clever woman was beyond her.

Meanwhile, Basil and his friends hunted to their heart's
content until finally, they made mention of heading back to
London. Cori figured that Basil had proven his independence

sufficiently for his taste and was ready again for the entertainment which could only be had in Town.

It was on the very day Basil announced his intent to depart that Cori saw Lord Arnett once again. He came to call, and Cori pulled Basil into the drawing room to add propriety. The men discussed the successes and pitfalls of the hunt at great length, forcing Cori to stifle not one, but two large yawns before the topic was changed to something of interest.

"I came to take my leave," Lord Arnett inserted after hearing that Basil and his party would soon be departing. "It appears I needn't have bothered, however, if we are all to travel to London."

"Not all. My sisters shall stay here." Basil's voice rang with such indifference, Cori felt like fading into the soft cushion behind her.

She had not been addressed once beyond the proper greeting since Lord Arnett's arrival in her drawing room. His eyes had remained fixed on Basil through the duration of their visit.

"My grandmother will appreciate that," Lord Arnett supplied.

Cori looked up and found him watching her. She would like to think it was with interest, but she had once seen the way he looked at Rose, and this was nothing like that. No, this was something entirely different. Pity, perhaps?

"I have found myself becoming quite fond of your grandmother," Cori said, with all the dignity she possessed.

"The feeling is mutual." Lord Arnett smiled, holding her gaze. "I shan't be gone long, Miss Cori, for a fortnight at most. There is too much to accomplish here to spend all of my time gallivanting across the world. Perhaps I may call when I return?"

Taken by surprise, she stammered, "W-why yes, of course."

She remained in a daze until the man left, and for the remainder of the day following. Whatever his sudden interest was, it had to be related to Rosemary somehow; there was no other explanation. Perhaps Lord Arnett wanted to get to know his future family? Yes, that must be it.

Cori fell asleep that night willing herself to see Lord Arnett the same way she saw Basil—as a brother, and nothing more. If only her heart would pay attention.

CHAPTER 5

*T*he carriage plodded along slowly as the London traffic moved at a snail's pace. Adam leaned back against the squabs and shut his eyes, hoping to ward off frustration. Every bit they moved forward was another moment closer to his reckoning.

"I do not know how I let you talk me into this," he said to his brother seated across from him.

"I do," Travis responded with levity. Adam did not need to open his eyes to know his brother was laughing. At his expense.

"Father wants an heir."

That opened his eyes. He was surprised to find Travis looking at him with a serious note in his usually mirthful expression. Adam swallowed the sawdust lump that formed in his throat. Travis was right; Father was the reason he was back in this horrid town on his way to a dreadful ball. On his way to see *her*.

"That is an easy enough task to accomplish," he said with a feigned lightness he did not feel. "I shall propose to the first miss I come across, procure a special license and be married by sunrise.

"While I commend your eagerness to do Father's bidding, I suggest you at least find a woman who can fill Mama's shoes."

"And we've come to the sticking point." Adam leaned back in his seat again and resumed the bored air which came to him so easily. He could not pick just any woman. As a future Marquess and a current Earl, he had to choose a wife who could fill the responsibilities that came with those roles. While his title at present was a mere formality, the title of Marquess was all too real. And it would be his entirely too soon.

The carriage rumbled to a stop and Travis hopped out, not waiting for the footman to open the door and let down the step. Adam followed his brother at a more sedate pace, securing the bored elegance which would shield him for the evening. It was an easy persona to play, for it was how he felt most of the time. In fact, he could not quite remember the last time he felt anything other than the strain and weight of his responsibilities.

No, he could. It was scarce but a week ago when he ran to the aid of the Featherbottom girl. A smile touched his lips at the memory. He clearly remembered feeling the need to help her, and when she came into sight and he saw the dog on top of her, his fear was realized. Thank heavens the threat was not as he had thought.

He had been angry at first to be so deceived, but it melted away by her surprisingly artless demeanor. He saw nothing of Rosemary in her younger sister. No, the younger one wore her heart on her sleeve. He could easily see the emotions pass over her face. Surprise, embarrassment, the moment she seemed sour... he would really like to know what she had been thinking then. In truth, he found her quite amusing. She did not possess her sister's sheer beauty, but he still found himself asking to call on her again; it hadn't surprised him when he felt glad she had accepted. He could easily pursue a friendship with the girl; the thought buoyed him up, in spite of the task that lay before him.

The ball was halfway over by the time the Arnett brothers

arrived, and they entered the room at the precise moment the stringed instruments started the waltz. The supper dance, to be sure. The one Rosemary told him she would keep for him when they passed one another at the park earlier. The brazen girl was smart. He was too much a gentleman to refuse. He had half hoped he would arrive too late for the dance in order to prove to her—and himself—that she held no power over him, but the rebellious half of him looked forward to it with anticipation.

It took only a moment to locate her standing beside her mother. She shone like a clear beacon. Making his way through the crowds, they parted like the Red Sea. It was laughable how highly expected their union was among high society. Apparently, no one expected him to have any self-respect. Himself included, it seemed.

He bowed to Mrs. Featherbottom first. "Your servant," he mumbled over her hand. He turned to Rosemary, overcome by her striking figure in the elegant ball gown. She was brilliant, he conceded, for she never went as far as others did, dampening their skirts or lowering their décolletage. She remained regal and much like...well, much like a Marchioness.

He led her out onto the dance floor, quite aware of the eyes following them. The expectation was palpable and brought a thin sheen of sweat to his brow. He looked down into Rosemary's coy smile and full eyes. The expectation there roiled his gut. Swallowing bile, he swung the beauty around, answering her questions simply and trying to remain composed. Her hand tightened in his, forcing him to look at her again. Her slender eyebrows raised slightly, a gently confused look gracing her perfect features.

"You seem distracted tonight, my lord," she said in a soft, willowy voice. Onlookers would believe them to be in a private *tête-à-tête*, so he simply looked away, continuing the dance, careful to keep his bored expression solid and unwavering.

"I am a busy man," he responded eventually.

"Of course," she agreed. "You wish for things to be settled."

He could not help the infinitesimal raising of his own brows. That was bold, indeed.

"As does your father," she continued.

Adam was ready to drop her hands and walk away, but she would never survive the scandal. That shouldn't tempt him, and yet...

"I am not one to like to wait either, my lord."

"No, you aren't, are you?" he said, finally looking into her clear blue eyes. He had startled her. Their reacquaintance of the previous few weeks was a natural proceeding that mimicked their original courtship. Yet, neither of them had brought up the courtship of a year and a half ago, or the subsequent betrothal between Rosemary and Adam's good friend, Lord Hammond.

The music ended and he returned Rosemary to her mother, bowing with poise and grace belying the seething he felt in his bones. He could see the panic in Rosemary's eyes and enjoyed it for a moment longer before turning away and crossing out the door. He saluted a surprised Travis on his way out and waved off the footman who offered to call for his carriage. A nice, brisk walk would do him some good.

At that moment he wanted nothing more than to be finished with this business. On that count, she had been right. But the idea of marrying Rosemary soured his stomach and he realized it was the last thing he wanted. He walked the dark streets, passing a carriage here and there, an occasional house lit up with lights and music, and he longed for his simple country life. He yearned for it, in fact, much like he had the entire year he'd spent abroad.

Coming to a sharp stop, he made a decision. He owed Rosemary nothing. If she was so desperate to be wed, then so be it. She could have her pick of the bachelors in London.

He was going home.

CHAPTER 6

*C*ori said farewell to the lively Dowager Marchioness and skipped away. She was beginning to grow fond of the spritely old woman with her bizarre trinkets and multitude of exotic fowls with their squawking voices and brilliant colors; especially the green parrot she had taught to mimic her own voice. The Dowager Lady Berwind was quite the character, but the words used to describe her by her daughter-in-law made Cori feel ill. The older woman was not vulgar, rude, or boorish in the least. And neither was she high in the instep, for she had just spent the last hour learning what she could from Cori in regard to cultivating her vegetable garden.

For a woman with a small army of servants at her disposal, she laid claim to a good variety of knowledge. Cori felt a kinship with the dowager and vowed to remain her consistent visitor, regardless of what happened when the Arnett family returned to residence. The dower house was a good way removed from Windfall; the Arnetts would not complain about Cori's regular visits, for they probably would not even know about them.

But what was she thinking? Lady Berwind would probably

consider it a favor. Was she not the very one who requested Cori to visit in the first place?

Swinging her basket, Cori wound her way down the embankment toward the creek lined with brambles of blackberries. She was still on Arnett property, but the dowager had given her express permission and she was ready to fill her stomach with ripe, juicy berries and hopefully, if Cook agreed, a pie later.

Pulling her old, smudged gardening apron from the basket, Cori tied the laces behind her back and proceeded to search the bushes for berries. This late in the season the bushes were picked over, but high at the top were the juiciest, ripest berries she had ever seen. It was such a pity they grew so beautifully in the one place they would never be reached. She continued along the blackberries, slowly filling her basket until she reached a particular spot overflowing with perfect, pie-ready berries. She stretched on her toes, nearly swiping the hanging fruit with the tips of her fingers.

Taking a step back, Cori admired the unreachable fruit until her vision alighted on something right behind it.

No, dare she?

A moment later, her mind made up, Cori rounded the brambles until she reached the opposite side. A large oak tree loomed over the berries, shading one section of the bushes. The shaded area had not yielded much fruit, but just to its left was a patch full to the brim of large, ripe berries. If she could only get onto that particular branch, she would have her basket full in the snap of a finger.

She removed her half boots and stockings and hid them beneath a section of the blackberry bush—she remembered that finding purchase on the branches had always been easier with bare feet—then swung the basket over her shoulder and began to climb. Not two minutes later Cori found herself sitting on the branch directly beside the monstrously tall brambles and picking sweet, sun-ripened berries. Her basket was full to over-flowing just as she predicted, and she hung it over a nearby branch, enjoying the view from up high. She had stayed at The Dowager's house longer than she anticipated and was cutting into tea time, but the exquisite berries were doing a splendid job in its place.

She popped one particularly large berry into her mouth and moaned quietly as the flavor erupted on her tongue.

"You make the berries look so divine, I have half a mind to join you up there."

ADAM COULD TELL he'd shocked her by the way her eyes flew open and the blood drained from her face. Achievement at his paltry accomplishment coursed through him and he worked hard to keep the grin on his face contained. She looked like a ragamuffin child, perched on the branch and stuffing her mouth with berries, her shockingly bare feet dangling.

"I have permission," Miss Featherbottom defended. He could see the streak of stubbornness that undoubtedly coursed through her.

"I have not come to chastise you." In fact, he did not know why he'd come at all. Only that since returning home an hour previously he'd had the urge to visit the creek. Not something he had previously been wont to do.

"Why have you come?" she asked cautiously. She remained still, he noticed. Unmoved from her perch up high.

"To the blackberry bushes on my own land?" He accompa-nied the remark with a lifted brow, let her make of it what she would. She did not need to know he was merely passing by to get to their spot at the creek.

"I apologize for my impertinence, my lord. If you would only avert your eyes…" She had trailed off, but he knew what she was getting at. And why she was still up on the branch.

"You don't wish for any assistance?" He could not help but tease. He liked to watch her squirm, as it was so very genuine. How had he thought of her previously? Oh, right. Artless.

The look she gave him was so dry he could not help the laugh he barked out. He turned his back on her, raising his arms in surrender. A moment passed and he listened to the rustling of the leaves and branches above him. A thud indicated that she had jumped down.

"Stay," she commanded. He was so surprised by the candid order that he obeyed. He was not used to being told what to do in such a way. He turned his head slowly in time to see her lower her skirts.

"Do you always take your shoes off when climbing trees?" he asked with his back still turned. Part of him regretted not waiting to voice the remark, for he would have liked to see her expression when he said it.

"Ask your brother," she retorted, coming around him with a basket full to the brim with ripe, juicy blackberries. "Until this moment he is the only person I have climbed with. He taught me, in fact."

Her words released an unwelcome feeling. But a feeling of what, he could not tell.

"Are you going to share?"

She faced him fully and gave him an impish smile. Her lips were stained dark, no doubt from the berries, and he found himself drawn to them. Until she spoke.

"Your grandmother did not mention your impending return."

"She did not know." Adam fell into step beside her as she hooked the basket over her arm and began walking along the creekside. "Have you recently been to visit her?"

"Yes, today we were gardening." She gestured to her stained apron over a serviceable gray gown. Most likely the one she wore for outdoor pursuits. Such as gardening. And berry-picking.

"I see her most days, in fact. The Dowager Lady Berwind is quite an amazing woman."

He smiled at her then and she faltered when their gazes met. He shot out an arm to steady her and she smiled her thanks before carefully removing herself from his grasp. Strange, that. Women usually loved it when he guided them by the arm.

Clearing her throat delicately, she trained her gaze straight ahead. "Have you completed your business in Town?"

"In a sense," he answered. She could not know he was planning to remove himself from the acquaintance of her family indefinitely. He had to if he was ever going to escape Rosemary's artful ways. It was a pity. He liked Mr. Featherbottom excessively, and this little minx was growing on him. If only he could remember her name.

"I assume Windfall is happy to have you, my lord. Your father in particular."

"What do you know of my father?" he asked, bristling. The Marquess was a sore subject.

"Only that he is ailing. We sent over a few herbs my father swears by, but I understand at this point the doctor's main motive is to keep the Marquess comfortable."

"Yes, that would be correct," he said stiffly. He should have known she would only have his father's health concerns in mind. "He grows weaker by the day I am afraid, Miss Featherbottom."

"That is my sister. Really, you must call me Miss Cori."

Cori. That was it. "Right," he agreed. "My mistake. Tell me, does your governess often let you roam alone, Miss Cori?"

She looked up at him with such surprise and indignation that he nearly chuckled. "At twenty years of age I hardly have use or requirement of a governess, my lord."

He was taken back.

"Twenty, and still here in the country?" he asked, astonished. He had assumed her to be fifteen, sixteen at the most. Twenty was nearly on the shelf by London's standards. What was she doing wasting away in the country?

"Yes, I am twenty and have yet to have a season. Please, do not refine too much upon it. Once my sister marries, I will have ample opportunities."

So that was it. They planned on Rosemary making a match that would pave the way for the rest of her siblings. Adam found himself resenting Rosemary more and more. She had found success during her first season, and even more at her second. The only reason she had waited so long to accept any hand in marriage was because she had enjoyed playing the game. And he had foolishly sat by and let her. Little did he know she had a sister waiting at home for her own turn.

He turned and took in the woman walking beside him. She was average in height and figure, with an oval face dusted by freckles and a set of beautifully curved eyebrows. She must have felt his gaze for a blush spread enticingly over her cheeks and her dark, ample lashes fanned out as she cast her eyes down. She was prettier than he had first noticed.

"Has Lord Travis returned with you?" she asked.

Adam cleared his throat and watched as they came upon the crossing place. The creek was low here and the rocks high enough that crossing the water could be accomplished easily while remaining dry. He watched her skip across and swiftly followed before offering his arm on the other side of the creek bed. He could see she was hesitant to accept his chivalrous offer so he swooped the basket off of her arm and placed her hand within his bent elbow. She did not demur, and he counted it a success.

"Travis stayed behind."

She nodded.

He found himself wanting to tell her all about the dinners

and balls he attended, particularly the final one where he left Rosemary and walked out. He would have liked to know how London society reacted but had been too eager to make his escape. Now, he wanted to see Cori's reaction, hear her opinions. But that was strange. Instead, he settled for asking about her.

"And how do you spend your days, Miss Cori?"

"I should tell you that I practice the pianoforte until I can play it flawlessly and then embroider pillows and paint screens, but it is untrue and too boring by half." She laughed and he found himself reacting to her in the strangest way, drawn to the melodic sound.

"Then what do you do instead?" He could not hide the amusement he felt. Nor, he found, did he want to.

"People. I like to visit with people."

He conjured up an image of a gossiping Cori and immediately slashed it from his mind.

"I visit your grandmother daily, at least, and then there are some of the other neighbors, my sisters, when they are not occupied, or the sick families in the village who need assistance. I am no saint, but I try to take them soup and bread when I can."

"And blackberry tarts?"

"Oh, no, sir! These shall never be turned into tarts."

Her vehemence made him laugh. "You plan to eat them all?"

She gave him a sideways smile and he could not help the grin that stretched his lips and pushed up his cheeks. "A pie, my lord. The most delicious way to eat blackberries."

"And quite a bit more difficult to share."

"Unless there are more than one," she said thoughtfully.

They reached the rear side of the Featherbottom's house and he was reluctant to let her go. She slipped her hand from his arm and waited expectantly. "If I return your basket, Miss Cori, am I to be one of the fortunate few to enjoy a slice of pie?"

"We shall see how many of those berries make it into the kitchen, won't we?"

He barked a laugh and returned the basket before bowing and turning away. It was not until he reached Windfall again that he realized he had smiled the whole walk home.

CHAPTER 7

*a*dam read the note several times before chucking it in the fire. He should thank Travis for warning him, but really, he was too angry to feel anything beyond indignation at the moment. It was beyond him why his mother promoted the match with Rosemary Featherbottom. She came from impeccable lineage and a comfortable country estate, her father a pillar in the political community, but that was where her attributes ceased. She did not have a fortune for a dowry and nowhere could her family claim legitimate relations with the titled aristocracy. Of course, he did not lack for either commodity, his family rich in both money and titles, but still.

It had to do with his father, he decided. His Mama must be as desperate as Father to see him wed and an heir in place. If Father—heaven forbid—was to pass before he married, then he'd have to wait a year before marrying at all. He found himself wishing for that safeguard. But of course, he'd never want it at the expense of his parent, or the other responsibilities which would come with it.

He swirled the brandy in his glass, ruminating over his

dilemma. Rosemary was on her way home. Within a day or two she would be in residence not five miles away, less than two if one did not use the roads. With his own mother coming home and bringing his sister, it was only a matter of time before Rosemary became a permanent fixture in his home once again.

He stood abruptly, startling Nieves.

"I apologize, my lord," the butler said. "I was only bringing in some refreshment."

"I have no appetite," Adam grumbled.

"Very good, sir. Only…"

Adam waited for the stately butler to continue, but he did not. He sighed. "Yes, Nieves?"

"The neighbor sent over this pie specifically for your lordship and since it is still warm, I assumed you'd appreciate a fresh piece."

He perked up. "A pie?"

"Yes, my lord."

"Very well," he conceded. The butler placed a plate on the table beside him with a fresh slice of blackberry pie and a fork. Nieves took himself off and Adam pulled the plate onto his lap before digging in.

The pie was heaven. A knock interrupted his enjoyment and he called entrance. Nieves approached him with a small note. "This was delivered with the pie, my lord. I forgot it on the tray."

Adam took the note and gestured that he did not need anything else. As soon as the door closed he shoved another bite into his mouth and tore open the seal.

Lord Arnett-

As it turns out, there were plenty of berries for multiple pies. Do not fret yourself, for I have made enough to serve not only my household and yours, but another neighbor as well.

-C

ADAM SMILED around his final bite. Then he choked slightly when he reread the note. *Cori* made the pie? That was as ludicrous as it was believable. His gaze lingered where she had signed the card. The simple "C" was elegant and effortless. And cunning, since she truly should not be caught sending a man clandestine notes to whom she was not engaged. He chuckled at her forthrightness, and then more so when he realized she was just being herself: a thoughtful neighbor.

He was out the door and ordering his stallion saddled before he knew what came over him. His mother and Rosemary were on their way to trap him.

Well, not if he had anything to say about it.

CORI REBRAIDED her hair and twisted it into a bun at the nape of her neck. She knew the hairstyle was quite severe, but it was low enough that her riding hat would not have to be pushed to the side. She picked up the skirts of her habit and threw them over her arm before leaving her room, nearly running into Harvey on the landing.

"My apologies, Miss Cori. I only wanted to inform you that you have a caller."

"Thank you, Harvey." Cori wondered who it could be. She made it to the door of the morning room before recalling that she was dressed in her riding habit. She could go change, but it was most likely the Vicar's wife, and Mrs. Neeson did not stand on ceremony with her.

Entering the morning room, she immediately wished she had indeed changed.

Lord Arnett turned from where he paced near the window. He bowed to her slightly; she curtsied back.

An awkward beat of silence consumed the room before she moved to the stuffed chairs beside the unlit fireplace. "Would you care to be seated, my lord?" She had left the door open for propriety's sake and she noticed the earl looking at it for a moment as if he wanted to cross the room and close it—or run through it. Instead he took the chair opposite her. The very one his mother had inhabited nearly a month prior.

"I should like to thank you for the pie, but more than that I need my curiosity satisfied."

"Yes?"

"Did you truly make it yourself?"

She felt the blush warm her cheeks. Had she written that? She tried to recall what she put in the inappropriate note but it was not coming to her. It had been a moment of whimsy to write it, but her pride had her wanting him to know exactly where the pie came from.

"I can see that you did. My compliments to the cook. It was delicious."

"Well, Cook did oversee the entire process. I never did know before what went into making a pie and I shall never eat one again without immense gratitude."

His smile was small and comfortable, and she found herself getting quite lost in it. His next words, however, pulled her abruptly from her dreamland in one brash swoop.

"Cori, will you marry me?"

Stunned, Cori was unaware of the man sitting beside her, chafing her hand in two of his own. He had apparently dragged his chair beside hers, for he had been much farther away moments earlier. She stood, pulling her hand from his, hastily putting space between them.

"You cannot be serious, sir, for you mean to offer for my sister."

"I mean to offer for the woman who I have offered for, and I believe it is you." There was an unmistakable edge to his voice, but Cori shoved it away. Surely he was confused. This could *not* be a marriage proposal.

"But you do not wish to marry me!" How could he not see that? What sort of game was he playing?

There was a firm set to his jaw as he rose, his hands clasped securely behind his back. "Should I beg approval from your father first, ma'am? Then shall you believe me?"

"Lord Arnett, I do not understand you." She knew she spoke quietly, but he must have heard her. His face softened and he approached her slowly as if she was a wild animal.

"Simply say yes," he said, "and do not try to understand me. I myself have long given up on trying to comprehend the female mind."

She took in his earnest expression. Had the man of her dreams truly proposed marriage? Of course, he never once said he loved her, but that was of little consequence.

Wasn't it?

Lord Arnett slowly took one of her hands in his own and squeezed her fingers softly. "It would make me the happiest of men if you would accept my suit."

She read his eyes for an ulterior motive, but came up short. He seemed so genuine, so honest, that she could not help but nod slowly. An answering grin spread across his face and her stomach did a bit of a tumble.

"I shall call on your father tomorrow and sort out the details. Should three weeks be enough time?"

"Three weeks?" she asked faintly.

He squeezed her hand and released it before leaning down and placing a chaste kiss on her cheek. Her body burned at the contact but he was halfway to the door before she registered his retreat. She hardly recalled herself saying farewell before he was gone. Moving to the windows, Cori watched him swing onto his horse and take off at a great speed and she found herself craving the same thing. She scoffed silently at herself before removing to the stables and Chance and the opportunity to sort out what had just happened while flying across the countryside.

If her mind settled on one indisputable fact, it was this: Rosemary was not going to be pleased.

CHAPTER 8

*T*he following month flew by in a mess of appointments, preparations, and avoidances. Her family had returned from London the day following the proposal and Lord Arnett arrived, as promised, to work out the marriage agreement with Mr. Featherbottom. Cori avoided announcing it to her family due to the very real possibility that she had dreamed up the scenario, but before she knew it, she was being whisked off to London to be fitted for a quick trousseau.

Rosemary scarce said one word to her since the fated day and she did not blame her. Mama had seemed confused and unsure, as if Lord Arnett was jesting and would call it off at any minute, but Papa continually reminded everyone he had the marriage agreement to prove it. There was no illusion. Lord Arnett intended to wed Cori.

Cori wondered what had taken place to inspire such confidence, but whatever it was, Papa was the only one who seemed confident in Lord Arnett's choice.

She saw Lord Arnett on two occasions following the proposal. Once when he came to dinner before she left for

London; an awkward affair where Rosemary glared daggers at Lord Arnett the entire time, intermixed with moments of scowling at Cori. Then once more at a betrothal dinner thrown for them by his mother in their London townhouse. He had ridden in for the occasion and then left the following morning, citing estate business.

After it all, Cori felt positive he was going to marry her, but less sure about whether or not he regretted his impulsive decision. At least, she assumed it was impulse. The man had come out of the blue with his desire to wed her and she had given into his demand with little consideration. Not that she would change her mind.

The wedding day dawned cloudy and gray. Cori was not one given to superstition, for they were in England after all and a cloudy day was quite normal, but she had hoped for a clear sky. The ceremony was a quick, small affair in Town. It was as she stood beside Lord Arnett that she realized what she had committed to: she was about to become a countess, a marchioness in the future. Swallowing past the lump of fear that formed, she pushed her way through the ceremony in a daze and the wedding breakfast shortly after.

Lord Arnett had not quite ignored her at the wedding breakfast, but neither was he overly attentive. Cori found herself standing beside a window looking onto the grassy square in front of Berwind House nursing a glass of lemonade. Her mother stood in the center of a flock of women, proudly describing the opulence of the estate, Windfall, which was to become Cori's home.

She startled when a silky voice spoke just above her ear. "A bit dazed, Lady Arnett?"

Turning to find Lord Travis beside her, she shot him a dry smile. "Yes, I am. How very strange to be called by that name."

He was surprised momentarily but recovered quickly. "I

should be used to your candor by now, but I am afraid you quite catch me off guard at times."

"Probably about as startled as I was to being referred to as Lady Arnett."

"You should get used to it," he said with a warm smile.

"I think I should like having another brother, Lord Travis," she said, returning his smile.

"Come now, you are my sister. You may drop the 'lord,' don't you think?"

"Likewise, you know."

"But I should never call you 'lord!'" Travis feigned shock.

Cori laughed, handing him her empty glass. "You could be a gentleman and dispose of my cup."

"I can and I will," he said, taking the cup and bowing away from her with a flourish. The man was positively delightful and she was glad he had been around the previous weeks to make her transition easier. If only the same could be said for her own family.

Rosemary stood a few paces away, her face a picture of calm reserve. She caught Cori's eye and the look of pure hatred displayed on her face was strong enough to send shivers down her spine.

Cori left the reception and found her way to the retiring room, needing a moment to catch her breath. Why she feared her sister was a mystery, for she was Lady Arnett now and nothing Rosemary did would alter that fact. She paced the room, forcing herself to take deep breaths until her calm was restored sufficiently to return to the reception. It was in her honor, after all.

"I would not envy her position," a voice said from around the corner.

"Nor I. How would you like to be married to a man who loves your own *sister*?"

Cori pulled up short, jumping into an alcove and pulling the drapes around her. She knew eavesdropping was unwise, but at present she could not help herself. She did not recognize the voices, but she had yet to join high society, so that was not surprising. One voice was thin and reedy, no doubt an older woman, but the other sounded youthful and full of spite.

"It is a done deal now, for in the eyes of the church Miss Featherbottom and his lordship are seen as brother and sister. Even if he divorced his new bride, he could never marry her sister."

"Whatever was he thinking in choosing the plain one? He could have had any bride he wished!"

The voices trailed away, accompanied by stifled giggles and guffaws, leaving Cori in an empty alcove void of more than just noise. She sat softly on the window seat behind her and considered what she had just heard. Her husband—*husband*—in love with Rosemary? She could not dispute their history. Indeed, she should have inquired about it further, perhaps, before accepting him.

But if he wanted to marry Rose then he would have asked her. He didn't.

A nagging feeling in the back of her mind reminded Cori that he never once pretended to love *her*. In fact, he had not even said he admired her. She was willing to marry him because of her long time infatuation and, to be honest, the shock of it all. In retrospect, she had quite lost her head. Her usually level, sensible head.

Oh, dear.

What had she done?

ADAM DOWNED another watery glass of lemonade and searched the room for his wife. His *wife*. A small smile tipped his lips at the thought. Not once since asking Cori had he regretted the impulse—for that is entirely what it was. He had left his house that morning with the idea of asking for her hand, and then seeing Cori elegant in her riding habit with the remnants of her pie on his taste buds utterly sold him.

He had spent the last month getting his affairs in order and working with his father's steward to right the wrongs which had accumulated while he gallivanted around Italy as his father remained laid up in bed. There was a lot of work yet, but he found that keeping himself busy made the time go by quickly, which he needed.

He regretted not spending much time with Cori prior to the wedding, but he knew she would understand. She was kind in that way. He remembered visiting with his grandmother to impart his news; her glowing approval had warmed his chest. He spent quite a bit of time with her in Italy before convincing her to move back to England and into the dower house, and her approval meant the world to him. It also reminded him he had indeed chosen the right Featherbottom daughter.

The main purposes of a wife, aside from producing an heir, would be to serve as a companion and help manage their social agenda and the estate. Clearly Cori would excel in that capacity.

If only he could locate her. Another sweep of the room proved him correct. She was not there. He had followed her with his eyes while doing his duty to speak to each and every guest, and the last place he saw her was near the window with Travis.

Come to think of it, he had not seen Travis in some time either. With furrowed brow, he begged pardon of the elderly gentleman he was speaking with and went into the hall. He saw two dainty feet swinging absently from a window seat and smiled. He should have known she would be drawn to the whimsical place.

"Escaping already?" he asked in a low voice.

She jumped at his approach and then quickly composed herself. She gave him a wan smile and he regretted immediately not being more diligent in remaining by her side during the wedding breakfast.

"Mind if I take a seat?" he asked, indicating the space beside her on the window seat.

She did not speak, but moved over to make room for him. Sitting beside her, he drew her hand into his own. She stared at their hands for a moment, her eyebrows pulling together in a semblance of a frown.

"What is troubling you?" he asked softly.

"Nothing," she replied with enthusiasm. She adeptly withdrew her hand from his and smiled brightly. Too brightly. "This whole day has been lovely. Your mother has quite outdone herself."

"Mother is not one to do things by half."

"Yes, quite so."

Adam was determined to get to the bottom of Cori's mood. "Are you feeling fatigued?"

"I suppose so."

"Then we should leave for Windfall at once."

"Oh, we are traveling tonight?" She looked disappointed.

"We don't have to," he relented. "I suppose we could get a good night of rest and take off first thing in the morning."

She gave him a genuine smile that made his stomach flip. His gaze rested on her lips. It would not be vulgar to close the distance between them now that they were wed.

Cori coughed, looking away from him and breaking the moment.

He was disappointed, but it was probably for the better. It would never do to be seen kissing one's wife at one's own wedding breakfast.

He offered his hand instead and she placed her shaky one within it before allowing him to pull her to a stand.

"On second thought," she said quietly as he led her toward the reception room. "I wouldn't mind leaving for the country right this moment."

Adam shot his bride a smile and squeezed her hand in his own. "Consider it done."

CHAPTER 9

he newly married couple bid their farewells and left for their country estate as quickly as a carriage could be summoned. Cori found herself avoiding Rosemary's blatant glare and wondering if Lord Arnett had ever kissed her. Well, of course he had. They were nearly engaged at one point, weren't they?

He had nearly kissed Cori when they sat in the window seat, hadn't he? If she had not coughed, he probably would have.

She found herself irritable and cross while the carriage bumped its way out of London; any attempt to pull her into conversation by her husband was for naught. They eventually lapsed into silence and spent the hours gazing out opposite windows. She fell asleep at one point and awoke with her forehead resting on Lord Arnett's shoulder, but she quickly extracted herself with a muttered apology.

By the time they arrived at Windfall, the couple was exhausted and went their separate ways gratefully. The housekeeper, Mrs. Banner, showed Cori to her room—pointing out the adjoining door to her husband's bedchamber—and sent a maid to help her undress and ready for bed. By the time she was tucked under the covers, the sleepless nights leading up to her wedding day culminated and she was quite asleep before her head fully settled into the pillow.

It was in the back of her mind that she must wait up for something but as quietly and unobtrusively as the thought came, it left her mind with equal stealth. Instead, she slept deep and long and dreamt of riding Chance through the fields, a pastime she had not had opportunity to truly partake in since becoming engaged a month prior.

ADAM PACED before the adjoining room door for nearly an hour before his curiosity got the best of him. He understood his wife was probably asleep at this point. She probably had been from the moment she stepped foot into her new bedchamber. But it was his wedding day, and all he wanted was a glimpse of her.

He took a deep breath and tried the door, relieved to find it unlocked. He chastised himself for second guessing her; in truth she probably had no idea it could lock from either side, but it felt like a success all the same. He opened the door cautiously, putting pressure on the door jamb to reduce the squeak of the hinges as he stepped inside.

A small candle burned on her bedside table. Left there by the maid, no doubt. He approached under the guise of blowing it out and took a moment to study his wife.

Cori laid in the center of the large canopied bed, curled on her side. Her mouth was slightly open as she breathed heavily, but her face was completely free of trouble. In fact, until that moment, he had not realized how troubled she had seemed earlier. Not at the wedding, but after he had found her in the alcove.

Sighing, he vowed to determine precisely what was bothering her. And, more to the point, he resolved to never again set foot within her bedchamber on his own accord. At least, not until he had been invited. He needed her to come to him.

But those were worries for another day. At present, he merely bent down and placed a feather light kiss on her temple before retreating to his own room and subsequently falling into a deep sleep.

CORI AWOKE CONFUSED. A vivid dream played with her memory of Lord Arnett kissing her forehead in the dark of the night. She shook her head to dislodge the delusion and looked about her. It took some time to place the rose silk wall hangings and matching bed canopy, but by the time her maid had finished starting the fire she remembered everything. Lord Arnett loving Rosemary; their escape to Windfall; that almost kiss. She found herself glad to be in familiar country and already began compiling a list of what she'd like to accomplish that day when she made her way down to breakfast.

She was surprised at first to find Lord Arnett seated at the breakfast table before her, standing when she entered the room. He was a busy man, taking great care in overseeing Windfall's estate business. Certainly that required an early start.

"Good morning," he said, reseating himself after she had taken a plate through the sideboard and filled it with a multitude of delicious items.

She nodded in response and took her own seat, sampling the berry jam on a slice of toasted bread. Delicious.

"Do you have a busy day ahead of you?" She ventured after a lengthy silence. That was the sort of thing married people spoke of at breakfast, was it not? She had never paid much attention before.

"Quite." He finished chewing before fixing her with a look.

"And yourself?"

"Yes." With more enthusiasm than she realized she had, Cori explained her plans to have Chance brought to the Windfall stables—as long as his lordship did not object, which he didn't—and then take herself to the dower house to visit with Grandmama—for now they were married she could well and truly call her that—and then meet with the housekeeper later to discuss the part Cori should play in learning to run such a large and well run house. It would help, she explained, that she was already of a slight acquaintance with Mrs. Banner and liked her immensely.

And she could not forget to check in with her sisters.

She looked up from this speech with sheepish eyes as she took in Lord Arnett's shocked expression. "Forgive me, my lord. Perhaps I should have inquired if you had a plan for me first."

He recovered himself nicely. "I should not presume to control the details of your day." He brought his fork down and played with the remnants of his breakfast absentmindedly. "Perhaps, though, it would be prudent to drop the titles since we are now husband and wife."

Cori was stunned. She knew many couples who called one another by their title instead of their given name and enjoyed long and happy marriages. She also was taken aback by his sudden shyness. It was not a side of Lord Arnett—Adam, she should think—she had ever before witnessed. He must have taken her surprise as a refusal for he stood abruptly and muttered something incohesive before fleeing for the door.

She never took him for a coward, either.

"Adam!" Cori called, effectively stopping him in his tracks. "I should like that above all things."

The pretty remark seemed to be the correct response. He smiled at her before bowing again and resuming his exit. Perhaps he'd had all the marital conversation he could manage for one day.

CHAPTER 10

*A*dam sat at his desk with his palms over his eyes, rubbing the sockets. Never before had he felt like such a bumbling fool. He had always had the charm and charisma of an older son set to inherit a fancy title and even fancier estate. His consequence had always been rather healthy, and his confidence even more so.

Until, of course, the incident...

He shook his head, careful not to think along those lines. A year on the continent had done wonders to regain his self esteem. Seeing Rosemary again had gone even farther in solidifying his resolve. He had thought marrying Cori would be the right thing. But then, after her mood alteration following the wedding, he began to fear he had made a mistake.

He stood suddenly, crossing to the study window and sweeping the lawn. Disappointment snaked through him. He had hoped to catch a glimpse of her. It was clear he did not fully understand women, let alone her. And it was even more obvious she had her own set of intricate feelings which he could not begin to comprehend.

It was time to set his focus on important matters of business. It was fortunate for Adam and his new wife that his family chose to remain behind in London for it would give him the opportunity he needed to settle into his role as a husband and get Cori situated in the house. It seemed, however, she was going to do just fine on her own.

He only hoped her efforts to involve herself in the household duties would not create tension with his mother when she returned.

Swallowing, Adam turned from the window. He sat at his desk and sifted through correspondence that had piled up while he was gone for the wedding festivities. He prepared paper and ink for responses. Retrieving his penknife, he trimmed his quill and watched the feather hover over vellum as he lost all thoughts. He tried to write a response but crumpled his efforts and tossed it into the fire grate.

Standing, Adam paced the dark Aubusson carpet. It was impossible to get any work done. All he could think about was Cori. And, if he was being honest, the kiss they almost shared following the wedding breakfast. He regretted not taking action. How would it have felt?

Clearly, he needed to get out of this office.

It was plain he needed to spend more time with his wife.

ADAM FOUND CORI'S HORSE, Chance, in the stables, happily munching away on his oats. He inquired with a stable hand and discovered that Cori had already come and gone that morning. He walked away feeling sheepish.

For all he knew, Cori valued her privacy and would find his searching her out objectionable.

He stopped halfway across the lawn. If Cori was with Mrs. Banner then he would let her be. If she was with his Grandmama, however, then it was perfectly acceptable to join their visit. He pivoted toward the dower house and found his long strides growing eager. If only he could snap out of it. Quite frankly, his interest was growing closer to obsession.

Shaking his head, he opened the gate and stepped into the front garden, his heart beating a rapid pattern against his chest. He heard a tinkling laugh through the open window.

Taking a deep breath, Adam poised to knock.

CHAPTER 11

*C*ori sipped her tea, the remnants of laughter lingering on her lips. Grandmama had insisted Cori use that particular title in addressing her, then set about asking questions about the fancy London wedding.

"When I married the Marquess," Grandmama began, her eyes closed as she reminisced, "I had the most exquisite gown. It would not be *de rigueur* today, but at the time it was the height of fashion. It was wide enough to fit four of me across in the skirt. And the sleeves! Oh dear, the sleeves were glorious."

"I am glad you loved your dress," Cori said, setting her tea cup on the low table in front of the sofa. "I am equally grateful that fashions have developed away from those horrid wire underthings."

"You little minx," Grandmama said, swatting at Cori with her fan. She returned to fanning herself, though why she felt so warm in the cool room was beyond Cori's understanding.

"And my grandson," she continued. "He cut quite a figure, I assume."

Cori's cheeks turned a delicate shade of pink. "Yes, he was quite handsome."

Grandmama gave her a knowing smile which only deepened the blush.

"Tell me," Cori said, clearing her throat delicately. "How does your garden go on?"

"Quite well, thank you. But you cannot change the subject so easily, my dear. I want to hear about the wedding. I have not seen the dashing young gentleman much since our return from the continent. Is he very much changed?"

"I shouldn't know," Cori responded, taking up her cup again to give her shaky fingers something to do. "I did not know him well before he left. It was my sister who claimed a relationship with him. One, I hear, which has been difficult for either of them to let go. However—"

A throat cleared loudly from behind and both women turned to find the subject of their conversation standing in the doorway. His red hair was disheveled and his eyes fairly glittered—though with humor or anger was anyone's guess.

"Be seated, dear," Grandmama said. "Don't stand about in the doorway gawking so. Would you care for tea?"

Adam chose a chair across from the women and accepted tea. He appeared stiff and formal, eyeing Cori warily. She did not understand the sudden intrusion, or the pointed scowl.

The silence stretched on and Cori gained enough courage to ask, "You have finished with your business?"

"Not hardly," he responded.

Her eyebrows rose in response and she had the desire to look away from his penetrating gaze. Instead she held it, sure there was some test or battle being performed and she was not going to fail.

"Is there a matter of urgency which brings you to my door?" Grandmama asked, her mouth growing firm.

Adam broke away, delivering a pitiful smile to his grandmother. "I simply wished to stop in and say hello."

Grandmama's expression clearly said she disbelieved him.

But it was no matter. Adam's behavior was strange. If he had come to see his Grandmama, then perhaps he wanted to do so alone. Cori had told him of her intentions to visit, but he could have forgotten. He clearly did not seem happy to see her there, that was for sure and certain.

Rising, Cori set her cup on the tray. "Thank you for tea, Grandmama. I have an appointment to keep with Mrs. Banner to go over the duties of the house and I should not be late."

"Come visit soon, dear," she said, rising to embrace Cori. "And a very welcome to our family."

Adam stood. "I will escort you back to the house."

Cori shot Grandmama a questioning glance, but she simply lifted her eyebrows in reply. It was a silent communication, enough for Cori to know that neither of them understood what was going on in the earl's mind to explain his odd behavior.

She wasn't particularly sure, either, that she wanted to find out.

Adam walked ahead in the front garden of the dower house and opened the gate for Cori, gesturing her through. When they reached the path that led them through the small wood toward the large lawn in front of the house, he offered his arm and Cori cautiously laid her hand there.

"Did you enjoy your visit?" he asked, his voice awkward and stilted.

"Yes, thank you."

They walked through the wood quietly. Cori thought to return the question, but his visit hadn't lasted so it did not really apply. Adam suddenly stopped before they reached the open, spanning lawn, and Cori halted in step.

"We have been invited to a ball," he said abruptly.

"Oh?"

"The Countess of Dunview is throwing one at the end of the month and sent a card expressly inviting me and my new bride.

I should like to attend." His eyes darted from hers to her lips and added, "If you are agreeable."

"I am agreeable," she said meekly.

Adam nodded once, his gaze slowly roaming her face. Her heart pounded against her chest as she held her breath. She could not tell if Adam was leaning closer or if it was in her imagination. She held still, fearing one slight movement would break the spell.

A sudden, loud barking pulled them from the moment. Anabelle burst from the trees, circling the pair in wild, yapping excitement.

Cori jumped. Adam suddenly stepped away, taking a slice of anticipation with him and replacing it with disappointment.

He turned away, an air of distraction about him.

"Did you come alone, girl?" Cori asked the dog, sweeping her gaze over the woods. She stepped onto the lawn to better survey the space. Adam stood nearby, watching the interaction.

"Cori!" a small voice yelled.

Her heart swelled when Marjie stepped from the trees, her blonde ringlets in disarray and her cheeks glowing.

"Have you come alone, you little imp?"

Marjie's smile grew. "Miss Hooplin doesn't mind."

Cori's eyebrow raised in question. She was unaware that Adam had come to stand behind her until he said, "Come to the house with us and we will send a note to your mother."

"My mother is still in London. But you may write to Miss Hooplin. When she wakes up, she might wonder where I am."

They started toward the house together. "And does she often nap?" Cori asked. The governess had been hired the moment Cori became engaged, for her mother could no longer rely on Cori to fill in where the missing governess lacked.

"Every day at the same time. So I take Annabelle out and we get our exercise. Miss Hooplin doesn't like exercise." She shrugged, her little mind unbothered. "Or dogs."

"What a strange creature she must be," Adam said dryly, watching Annabelle trot along beside Marjie.

Cori chuckled. It was Marjie's nature to do as she pleased, and even more so to be indifferent.

"How about a spot of tea and then I shall walk you home myself," Cori asked, pulling her sister in close.

"Lovely. But will you quit squeezing me, please?"

CHAPTER 12

*a*dam watched Cori mother her youngest sister with the greatest joy and satisfaction he had ever witnessed from a mother, natural or otherwise. More than he'd witnessed on his own, at any rate. He tried to give them privacy, leaving them alone in the parlor with their tea while he went to his study to care for his correspondence. But he quickly found he could not concentrate on writing letters with tinkling feminine laughter filtering down the hallway.

Drat Cori, and drat her little sister.

No, he did not truly feel that way. It was not their fault he had made a sort of game out of trying to guess which laughter belonged to which sister. He was fairly positive which one belonged to Cori when another sound came in that stumped him once more.

There was nothing else for it, he simply had to go and discover if he was correct or not.

Adam crossed the hallway, careful to enter the parlor right away. He did not want to make the mistake of lingering and hearing things better left unheard.

"Lord Arnett!" Marjie squealed. She was a fetching little

thing, and while she did not resemble Cori greatly in the obvious ways, her smile was identical. He found he liked her smile very much.

"Yes, you little rascal?"

Marjie giggled. "I have an idea for a game, but Cori refuses to play."

He looked at Cori. She was watching her younger sister with an indulgent smile. He was certain she would play anything Marjie asked.

"What game is that?"

"Archery!"

Adam chuckled. "I hate to bear the bad news, but that is not an idea for a new game."

"With Annabelle!" she continued enthusiastically.

Adam shot Cori a questioning glance and she explained, "The dog."

Oh. "You'd like to shoot your dog?" he asked, giving her the best haughty, judgmental look he could muster.

"Of course not," she said, unfazed. "I'd like to tie a target to her back. A moving target would be so challenging to hit!"

"Yes, I could see that." In truth, he admitted to himself, he wouldn't mind trying it either. But not at the expense of an animal.

"Shall we get you home now, dear?" Cori asked. "Your governess is surely awake by now and is likely expecting your return."

"That old hag couldn't see—"

"*Marjie.*" Cori reprimanded sternly. She evidently had experience using authority over her sister in such a way. "You will respect your governess."

"But you haven't met her," Marjie whined. "She really is horrid. And boring, Cori! She is so very boring."

Cori stood at once. It was apparent that she took responsibility for Marjie's poor manners and her blushing cheeks showed it. Adam found himself attracted to the Cori he was seeing. She was confident in the way she handled her sister, and even more so, she was competent.

For the first time in his life, Adam imagined a brood of little children running around, some with his red hair, others with Cori's dark brown. A mix of brown and green eyes watched their mother lovingly while she told them a bedtime story and tucked them into their cots. He was certain Cori would be the sort of mother who would insist on putting her own children to bed. A warmth spread through his chest. Clearly he had made a superb choice in a bride.

"I apologize," Marjie said, humbly curtseying before him. "I should not have spoken in such a crass manner. Please excuse my poor behavior."

Adam had trouble concealing the grin that stretched his lips. He nodded his acceptance and bowed before the child. "I hope you shall join us again soon, Miss Marjie."

She grinned before bouncing from the room.

"I shall return shortly," Cori said. "I cannot help but feel I ought to explain to the new governess why I allowed Marjie to remain for the afternoon instead of sending her home directly."

"Why did you allow her to stay?" Adam inquired, stepping closer and inhaling a faint floral scent.

Cori had an air of distraction about her. "I suppose it was selfish. I missed Marjie. I didn't see her at all while I was in London preparing for the wedding."

"A valid reason," Adam agreed.

Cori shot him a small grin before curtseying and quitting the room. Adam watched her go, the scent she left behind making him restless. He could not place exactly what she smelled of, but he vowed to discover it by the end of the week.

CHAPTER 13

*T*he house was the same as it had been a month prior, but Cori felt like a different person upon entering it. Marjie skipped ahead, unrepentant, and Cori felt a tinge of regret at allowing her to remain at Windfall for so long. She meant what she said to Adam, however. She had missed her sister and selfishly wanted a familiar presence in the new house. They were neighbors, after all.

"Marjie, you are to go to the school room this moment," a stern voice said crisply. Cori heard her sister mutter a reply.

"Hello, Miss Hooplin," she said, approaching the governess. "I am Cori Feather—Arnett. I apologize for Marjie's escape this afternoon. I fear we are unused to being separated. And I have not seen her these last few weeks."

"That is no excuse for uncivilized gallivanting across the neighbor's fields."

The woman had no sense of adventure. Or, it seemed, any flexibility.

Cori delivered a small smile, making an effort to be congenial. "Perhaps I can schedule a time to come and see my sisters, and then we can avoid any repeat indiscretions."

Miss Hooplin's mouth remained in a tight line, small wrinkles around her lips and eyes evidence of many years of distaste. Cori was beginning to understand the cause for Marjie's earlier use of the word hag, and immediately chastised herself for her unkind thoughts.

"Perhaps on Tuesday afternoons?" Cori offered.

"Very well," the governess agreed. "We may see. If they lose their privileges, however, I make no promises."

Cori nodded. "Whatever you think is best."

She turned to leave. She wished to see Meg, but asking Miss Hooplin would be pointless. The woman would no doubt wield her power and explain how Meg was not allowed visitors at present—or some other faulty excuse.

Instead, Cori made her way to the library, her sister's favorite hideaway, and was rewarded with the image of sea green skirts amidst the stacks of leather-bound books.

"Meg," Cori said quietly.

"Cori!" she replied, bounding up from her chair after carefully setting her book on the table beside it. She pulled her sister into an embrace, an uncommon occurrence to be sure. "How is marriage?" she asked.

"I am growing accustomed to it," Cori said with a shrug. "And I have just scheduled Tuesday afternoons for my visiting time with you and Marjie."

Meg did not inquire. She must have understood the necessity of scheduling time for visits with the new governess. Cori leaned in. "And how are things going with Miss Hooplin?"

"Well enough," Meg said lightly. "She is far stricter than either of us are used to. But that is not so horrible." She grinned suddenly. "Marjie could use some firm direction in her life."

Cori shared in the smile. "I better be off. I shall see you Tuesday, if not before."

"And don't forget the jonquil evening gown," Meg reminded

her, a cheeky smile on the younger girl's face. "I won it fair and square."

Cori leaned forward and kissed her sister's cheek before departing, hoping to hide the tears that sat in her eyes.

She made her way home, her mind full of the events of the day. One in particular was clouding her mind, and she could not shove it from her thoughts. Adam had clearly intended to kiss her earlier in the woods. That she welcomed the advance both frightened and angered her.

He was not in love with her, he'd made that clear. If what those gossiping women said was true, then she needed to wrap her mind around living with a husband who loved her sister. A difficult feat, to be sure. She had spent a lifetime feeling inferior to Rosemary. Her parents, her friends, and society as a whole esteemed Rosemary's graceful beauty highly and Cori would never measure up.

When she was a child, she had held onto the knowledge that someday, when she married and had a family of her own, at least *someone* would love and care for her more than they did Rosemary.

It would appear she was not going to be blessed in that way. Tears silently trailed down her cheeks and she used the back of her hand to dash them away.

She could not stay upset with Adam; it was not his fault he had fallen in love with Rosemary first. Neither was he to blame for Cori's naive expectations of a romantic marriage.

Cori simply had to find a way to come to terms with her new role and learn to embrace it.

CORI RETURNED HOME to a seemingly empty house. Drawn to the study door for no discernable reason aside from a desire to see the earl, she knocked lightly, waiting on the tips of her toes for his deep drawl. Silence met her, and she counted to ten quietly, counted backward, and then knocked again.

When no answer came a second time, she opened the door, quietly poking her head inside. A deserted desk surrounded by empty chairs faced her, and she slipped inside. Crossing to the desk, Cori trailed her fingers lightly along the carved mahogany border, taking in every bit of the room that might give her a hint about her new husband. The painted horses above the mantle were gloriously depicted mid jump, a clear indication of Adam's preference for a less sedate ride.

Stepping around the desk, she noted the stack of correspondence beside fresh paper, his organization evident in the clear piles and clean desktop. Glancing toward the door left ajar, the empty hallway visible, she opened the top drawer to the desk, inventorying the neat pens lined up beside sand and ink. She quietly perused the other drawers, impressed by Adams' clear sense of order.

The final drawer at the bottom stuck, and she had to yank to get it open. It was empty but for a narrow box. Lifting the box, a small feeling within her protested the invasion. This was no minor curiosity; whatever Adam had hidden away here was likely personal.

The moment Cori lifted the lid, she immediately regretted her actions but found there was no turning back. Rosemary's sloping scrawl lined the paper in her trembling hands. Jealousy swirled deep in her gut. She should look away, but she felt powerless, motivated by some feral need to see every word Rosemary had ever written him. She scanned the contents of the first missive as her stomach constricted.

It was a letter of affection, the date indicating its receipt long before Rosemary had ever accepted Lord Hammond's proposal.

Cori folded the letter and tucked it back in the box, opening the next, and then the next. They all contained the same devout exclamations, clear descriptions of their future together. The letters also contained consistent requests to delay their engagement because Rosemary's father wished for her to see London first.

It was evident that not only had Rosemary lied, but she had purposefully led Adam on before choosing another suitor entirely. Cori had always assumed her sister had behaved badly, but the blatant lies in her letters...it was far worse than she'd ever imagined. No wonder Adam felt so ruined.

Cori replaced the missives, closing the box and hiding it away in the drawer.

Fleeing the room, she berated her foolish actions. It was bad enough to assume he still loved Rosemary, to believe he'd only married her to increase his chances of seeing the Featherbottom sister he actually preferred. But this was far worse. Adam had clearly proposed to Cori out of spite. She was merely a pawn in his desire to wound Rosemary as badly as she had wounded him. Had he given no thought to how Rosemary would not be the only casualty of this faulty marriage?

For now Cori was wounded as well.

SHE CHANGED with the help of a maid and went down to meet Adam for dinner for the first time in their home together. She had thoroughly considered her discoveries in the study and came to a clear conclusion: she must guard her heart. She was married to Adam now, but she did not need to subject herself to further pain by leaving her heart unprotected.

"You look lovely," Adam said, coming to a stand when Cori stepped into the drawing room.

She gave him her hand, curtseying as he bent forth and kissed the back of her glove. Her cheeks warmed on their own accord and she clasped her hands before her, surreptitiously rubbing the place that burned from Adam's lips.

She glanced down at her pale pink gown, sure he was just being kind. The gown was one of Rosemary's castoffs. She had worn it a few times before discarding it, complaining about its style being thoroughly out of date. It suddenly occurred to Cori that Adam could have been to a dinner or card party where Rosemary wore this very gown. Did he remember it? Prefer her in it? She quickly dashed the poisonous thought from her mind.

Nieves announced dinner and Cori placed her hand lightly on Adam's arm, following him into the dining room. They sat at one end of the table, Adam at the head and Cori seated to his right.

"I thought it would be nice to sit close enough for conversation," he explained after seating Cori beside him. "I know you deserve the place on the other end of the table, but it is quite far away."

Cori glanced down the massive length of polished oak. She could see what he meant. If she had sat at the foot they would be quite far apart.

"Were you able to meet Miss Hooplin?" Adam asked, leaning back for a footman to place his dish before him on the table.

"Yes."

"And was she...?"

Cori looked at him expectantly. She assumed she already knew what he wanted to ask, but let the question dangle regardless. It was much more entertaining to see Adam squirm. She was positive she had never seen such a dignified lord squirm in all her life. And after her discovery in the study, she could abide giving Adam a little discomfort.

Adam cleared his throat. "The woman, I mean. The governess."

"Yes?" Cori asked innocently. "What about the governess?"

He leveled her with a look; she had been caught out. "You know perfectly well what I am trying to ask, you little minx. Now get on with it. How horrid was the ghastly governess?"

Cori grinned. "Marjie was spot on, I'm afraid. She was rather horrid indeed."

Concern marred his brow. "Perhaps we should intervene on her behalf?"

Returning her attention to her meal, she tried not to find his consideration attractive. She would not allow herself to misunderstand his concern to be anything other than it was. "I believe they will do just fine. I have been too lenient, truth be told, and both Meg and Marjie will benefit from stricter instruction." She chewed a bite of pork before continuing. "Miss Hooplin was likely so abrasive with me to assert her authority. I find I was taken aback at first, but she is in the right. I am not their governess, I am their sister. Now I get to enjoy the benefits of being a sister without the added discomfort of scolding."

"You shall cease your scolding?"

She glanced up. Adam was smiling down at her. It was an odd thing, she thought, to find one's husband was in fact agreeable. Before the wedding she had only imagined him steady and strong. That he had a sense of humor was certainly a bonus.

And confusing, at best.

Adam invited Cori to play for him after dinner and she was surprised when he followed her directly from the dining room instead of remaining behind for port. An hour was passed in front of the pianoforte and when Cori completed her final number, she rose, stretching her arms before her.

"Are you tired?" Adam asked.

It was on the tip of her tongue to scold him for his forwardness until she remembered he was her husband, to which she simply nodded.

"I can walk you upstairs," he offered. "But I am afraid I must return to my correspondence."

Cori was affronted. The man had gone back and forth from his study all day. From breakfast onward, whenever he wanted to get away he cited the need to write his letters. What man in

England—running an estate or otherwise—had the legitimate need to *correspond* all day?

"I can manage," Cori replied stiffly. She delivered a curtsey and walked from the room.

She could hardly blame the man for the past. Though he had acted rash and proposed to her in an effort to hurt Rosemary, she had acted rash and accepted the proposal. Love had a way of forcing people to do foolish things. But still, it was difficult to balance the feelings Adam ignited within her with the knowledge that he did not love her. She could not allow herself to fall for him more deeply than she already had when Rosemary held his heart; she just couldn't.

CHAPTER 14

he next few weeks passed quickly while Adam and Cori found a comfortable rhythm. They breakfasted every morning before going for a ride together. Then Cori would change and go about her bride visits, either accepting callers or spending her time with Grandmama in the dower cottage. Adam would go to his study and take care of necessary estate business until dinner. They would share a meal once more and then spend a comfortable evening in the drawing room with music or reading or light conversation, after which Cori would go up to bed and Adam would return to the study or library for a drink.

The schedule was consistent and reached the point of predictability. Neither of them had any complaints about the details of their day.

Except Adam, naturally, had suddenly realized how excessively boring estate business could be. He found himself at the window quite often, or pacing to the library and back in order to catch a glimpse of Cori and the guests she was entertaining at the time. He found himself wanting to be in the drawing room, until reason would take hold and he would discern that sitting through bride visits was exactly the last thing he wanted to do with his time.

He stood near his study window, arms crossed over his chest as he watched Cori walk across the lawn and enter the wooded path. She was visiting with Grandmama, no doubt. She did so nearly every day.

Adam had always had a special relationship with his grandmother and felt pride that his wife would maintain a connection with her as well. Though he should not feel surprise. He could not think of a single person who did not like Cori. The housekeeper adored her, the butler smiled at her fondly. Her sisters, obviously, worshipped her. She was special, of that he had no doubt.

Surprise filtered through him as he came to the conclusion that he cared for her, too. Deeply.

"The post, sir," Nieves said, holding out a silver platter with a few folded missives on top. Adam took the letters, halting at once when he noticed his brother's writing. Retrieving a penknife, he sliced through the wax seal of the first letter and unfolded the thick parchment. He read the contents, anger and irritation battling for precedence within him.

Drat his mother. His awful, meddlesome mother.

He glanced up, his gaze sweeping the lawn for a woman that he knew was no longer there. He needed to find her at once.

CORI STEPPED out of the dower cottage, rejuvenated by the conversation and companionship she always felt within it. Whether it was from a mutual love for gardening or a desire to see all pompous windbags removed from church pews on Sundays, Cori and Grandmama maintained a special kinship that had only strengthened when they became related.

She stepped through the front gate, warily watching the

ominous dark clouds rolling in. She had not noticed the poor weather when she set out earlier or she would have brought an umbrella. It was clearly going to rain.

A large figure stepped out in front of her and Cori screamed as large hands wrapped around her.

"It is only I!" he yelled, and she relaxed at once.

Stepping out of his hold she gave him a wary look, continuing toward the house. "Adam, what are you about? It is going to rain."

He caught up quickly, looking annoyed. "I needed to speak with you."

"We best get inside first."

He gripped her arm, pulling her around to face him. "I need to speak with you," he said, his eyes hard.

Fire flew through Cori. She refused to be handled in such a way. Ripping her arm from his grasp she leveled him with a look. The first drop fell from the sky, hitting her nose. She wiped it away with a finger. "Yes?"

Adam's eyes flitted up before landing on her again. He took her hand and pulled her forward, propelling her out of the wooded path as the rain began to fall.

They veered away from the house when they hit the open lawn and Cori tried to shout over the sudden onslaught of rain. "Where are we going? The house is that way!"

"The barn is closer!" he shouted back.

They made it through the large open door moments later, dripping and soaked through to the skin. Water pooled at their feet, already forming into puddles on the muddy barn floor.

"Would it not have been better to make a dash for the house?" Cori asked, wrapping her arms around herself and shivering.

"I was hoping we'd beat the majority of the rain," Adam said, pulling the door closed behind them. A horse nearby whinnied, upset from the rain, and the smell of manure lifted with the scent of wet earth.

The clouds had taken over the sky, blocking most of the sun and darkening the stables. Adam approached her slowly, his arms raised as though she was a mare in need of calming. "I apologize," he said. "I was thinking short term. It really does not sound like it is going to let up anytime soon."

"Perhaps it will," she said, moving past him to peek out the door. "Or perhaps it won't."

Adam came to stand so close behind her she could feel the body heat emanating from him onto her back. She stilled, unsure of how to handle the situation. He had seemed so bothered minutes before, and now he was merely conversational. It was a drastic change, one she had not seen in him before.

"I believe you are right. It appears as though it will rain for some time. I suppose we ought to make a run for the house."

Cori turned to look at Adam and found him closer than she imagined. His red hair was wet, water drops clinging to the ends, and his cravat was a soggy mess. She smiled despite herself at his unkempt appearance, realizing she must be equally disheveled.

"What is it?" he asked, his voice low.

Cori shook her head. "I am merely admiring your cravat."

He glanced down and a few drops of water fell from his head onto her cheek. His hand immediately came up to wipe them away, his fingers lingering on her jaw. She found herself holding her breath, the intensity in his eyes calling to her and pulling her in. She leaned forward of her own accord, her lips nearing his.

His mouth curved into a delectable smile and his gaze flitted to her mouth. His hands came around her waist, pulling her closer to him, when a loud bang hit the back wall of the barn and the couple jumped apart.

"The wind," Adam said, jogging across the barn to pull the

opposite door closed. Rain came in sideways, flooding him while he worked.

Cori watched him struggle with the door. Confused, she stepped back and leaned against the wall. This was not how a man acted who was in love with another woman. He had regarded her with such warmth and intensity. He'd held her waist so firm and gentle.

Slipping through the front door she ran through the rain, fighting the wind to reach the house. Rainwater trailed down her face, her jaw burning where Adam had caressed her earlier.

It was ridiculous that she allowed herself to become wrapped up in his arms—both literally and figuratively. The man did not care for her beyond friendship and the qualities she brought to the marriage. If she succumbed to his attractions, then he would survive. It was Cori who would come away crushed.

Wouldn't she?

Doubt crept in, but she did her best to evade it.

She made it into the foyer, slamming the door closed against the wind and dripping onto the marble floor. She requested a bath to be sent up at once and climbed the stairs with haste. She wanted to get away before Adam made it inside.

She needed to be alone.

CHAPTER 15

*A*dam paced the carpet of the breakfast room. He had never been so concerned with an answer to a question in all his life. The door opened and he halted, disappointed to find the maid returned, a small shake to her head.

"What did she say?" he asked sharply.

"Her maid said she took a tray in her room."

Adam groaned. He wanted to spend time with her. He needed to. Not only did he want to assure himself that she was all right, he was never going to break through the barrier Cori erected around herself without knowing her better.

He had spent his entire life watching a loveless marriage operate an estate, massive social agenda and parliament. He had thought he knew what he wanted in a wife when he proposed; a companion to manage the household and social engagements while he maintained his duties to the King. It was clear when he chose her that Cori was a thoughtful, elegant woman who would fill the role to perfection.

What he hadn't counted on was the caring.

Adam cared, deeply, about what Cori thought. He wanted to

know where she was and with whom she was spending her time.

He was not afraid to admit to himself that he was falling in love with his wife.

The letter he had received the day before only made things more complicated, and Adam felt it important to discuss the situation before anything could happen to ruin the progress they had made the last few weeks.

If nothing else, he needed to prepare her.

"Shall I retrieve her?" the maid asked, looking at Adam with mild curiosity.

"No. That is all." He dismissed her, filling a plate haphazardly at the sidebar and sitting down to eat, unsure of what he was spooning into his mouth. His only goal was nutrients at present, and then he would be able to consider the matter at hand and the best way to go about correcting it.

He could enter her bedchamber, but that would break the code he had set for himself after that very first night: he needed her to come to him.

"Blast it!" he said, startling the footman poised against the wall. He ran a hand over his face and stood, marching toward the stairs. Forget the code. He needed to talk to his wife, and he was going to talk to her now.

CORI LOOKED over her shoulder at the large, imposing estate and wondered if Adam could see her from the breakfast room as she rode away. Slipping out of the house had felt so cowardly, but she needed some time away. She clicked her tongue and Chance took off, jogging over the familiar, wet terrain. She was unsure if her solo ride would cause discord with her husband. While it was true that they had fallen into the routine of riding together following breakfast, they had never explicitly made it a daily plan.

And at present, Cori merely wanted to see her sisters.

She felt at once that something was different when she rode up to the stables and left Chance with Tim, her parent's groom. Crossing the muddy earth she stepped up to the front door and Harvey opened it, letting her into the foyer.

"Cori! What are you doing here?" her mother asked from the top of the staircase, her face a perfect picture of surprise.

"I have come to see Meg and Marjie. I did not realize you would be home."

Mother began descending the stairs. "They are up in the school room, but I suppose you are welcome to see them." She appeared wary and Cori was not at all sure why. The last she'd seen her mother, she was overjoyed at the superb match Cori had made. It had been foolish of her, perhaps, but she felt like she had finally made her mother proud.

She glanced up to the sour, pinched face her mother had so often given her and sighed. She did not look like a proud mother one bit.

Cori bid her mother farewell and mounted the stairs, eager to be in the schoolroom and regain some normalcy. She discovered her youngest sisters writing while their governess sat at the front of the room. All three of them turned when she opened the door.

"I apologize for the intrusion. I only came to say hello."

"It is not Tuesday," Miss Hooplin replied.

"Yes, it is not Tuesday."

"May we have a short break?" Marjie asked, her angelic face beseeching her governess.

The older woman looked from Cori to her sisters and said, "Five minutes, and not a moment more." She stepped from the room and Cori heard a door close down the hall.

"What is it?" Meg asked, her pale eyebrows drawn together.

Cori shrugged, coming to sit near them. "I missed you."

"Of course you did!" Marjie squealed, coming to snuggle on her lap. Cori put her arms around her youngest sister, holding her close for a moment as though her warmth and exuberance would chase away the melancholy. Would she ever have children of her own? Or would Meg and Marjie be the closest she ever felt to mothering? It was impossible not to feel a thread of rejection that Adam had yet to visit her room. She could only hope the matter would correct itself in time.

Biting back tears, she shook her head. "I do not know why I am so emotional. Perhaps it is just that marriage is not quite what I had anticipated."

"How is marriage then?" a voice asked from the doorway. Cori glanced up sharply to see Rosemary stepping into the room. Her face was drawn; her eyes looked tired.

"Hello, Rose," Cori said, eliciting a scowl from her sister.

"Looking forward to spending some quality time together?" Rosemary asked before smiling like a feline and slinking away. It was clear their relationship had a long way to go before it would mend. If, indeed, it ever did.

"Don't mind her," Meg said. "She is still licking her wounds. I don't think she understands how you were able to steal Lord Arnett from her."

"I didn't *steal* anyone!" Cori nearly yelled, affronted. "He approached me. Wait..." She eyed Meg and Marjie, then continued. "Does everything think that is what I did? Steal Adam from my sister? Does no one understand it was he who pursued me? That he proposed to her first?"

Meg and Marjie's innocent expressions said more than words ever could. Mortification filtered through Cori's body, stunning her. Of course she knew Rosemary desired Adam for a husband after Lord Hammond's death; both she and their mother had made that very clear. But Rose had refused his proposal, and Cori did not go out of her way to *take* Adam, she had simply agreed to be his wife. What she questioned now, was whether she would have made the same decision if she'd known before what she knew now: that he had deeply loved her sister, and only married her out of spite.

After a moment, she stood. She needed to remove herself from her former home.

"Where are you going?" Marjie asked, disappointed.

"Home—er, well. Away. I need to get away."

Cori fled the house, unsure if anyone watched her retreat. She jumped onto Chance's back and flew from the stables faster than was safe, the ground wet from the previous day's rain.

She approached the jump—the hedge her father deemed unsafe. Deciding in a moment so quick she did not consciously claim it, she turned Chance toward the hedge, gripping her tightly, tensing herself for flight.

She leapt obediently into the air, and it was as glorious as it was terrifying. The moment Chance's hooves hit the ground she rocked forward, gasping for breath and laughing at the madness of it. Her father was right, it was unsafe and she had nearly not cleared the hedge. But, she did it. And the exhilaration filling her was a cure for her melancholy like nothing before.

A horse came into view and she recognized the man's flaming red hair at once. Her mood shifted, irritated that he had come after her. Cori turned Chance for the back fields of her parents' home and let the mare have her head. She could faintly hear Adam calling to her, but ignored him, eager to be alone. She had only just regained some composure and Adam had the power to undo it again.

Chance was fast, but Adam's horse was faster. He caught up to her within minutes, reaching out to grab hold of her horse's bridle. She resented his manhandling and glared at him. "I will slow," she called, forcing him to release her horse.

Chance came to a stop, chest heaving in time with Cori's.

Adam was glowering. "What was that for? Do you realize

how dangerous that jump was with all this mud?" he shouted, jumping from his horse. He came around to pull her down and she unhooked her leg just in time to avoid a painful dismount.

He set her roughly on the ground and she nearly toppled, heavy mud squelching beneath her boots. She had enough of Adam's high-handed treatment of her. Blood boiling, she registered the fire in his eyes, sure it matched her own.

"I was fully capable of jumping that hedge, clearly. And I desired some *solitude*," she said finally, chest heaving.

He looked shocked. "Whatever did I do?"

Cori turned from him. Stomping away from her husband and their horses in a thoroughly flooded field, effectively ruining the hem of her favorite riding habit.

"Cori, stop," he said, grabbing her arm.

She wrenched it free of his grip. "Must you always do that?" she shouted.

He reared back as though he'd been slapped.

"You needn't grab me," she said, softening her tone.

"I apologize," he said stiffly. "I was unaware."

Cori searched his gaze, surprised to find him genuine. Why must they argue? She was so defeated, so unsure of everything: herself, her marriage, her place in the house and now within society. She was a lone island amidst many moving ships and she merely wished to understand whether the ships were friends or traitors.

Adam spoke, softer now. "I apologize if I've hurt you." His clear eyes regarded her closely and she was suddenly overcome with doubt. The women who had gossiped at her wedding and the letters she had found in the drawer proved how unfaithful Adam's heart had been, but the way he looked at her now told an entirely different story.

Tears sprang to her eyes and she looked to the sky, wishing them away. Adam's hand moved to wipe them away but he halted, hesitating before dropping his hand again.

That action hurt her more than any previous words. She had driven another wedge between their already rocky relationship.

"May we begin anew?" she asked.

"What do you mean?"

Cori took a deep breath. It had to be everything, or it would achieve nothing. She needed to lay her doubts and insecurities at his feet and leave them for him to do with what he would. Their marriage would not be able to thrive otherwise.

"What I mean is, may we pretend today is the first day? This is the first moment for us. There is no preexisting relationship between our families; you have never met Rosemary."

He winced and she faltered.

Gathering courage, she continued, her voice laced with tears. "I am ordinary, that I know, but I can be a good wife if you will allow me the time to prove myself. You needn't always hide away and write your letters. You may trust me with details of estate business or whatever else worries you. I can be your confidant and friend. If nothing more, Adam, I can be your friend."

He searched her face, his shoulders slumped forward. "You are not ordinary, Cori Arnett. Indeed, you are far from ordinary."

He swept her into his arms, claiming her lips with a passion she had never before imagined. She slid her hands up to grip his lapel and returned the kiss, hopeful for the message it brought.

Moments later he leaned his head back, resting his forehead on hers. "I was never in love with your sister," he said. Cori tried to step back, but he held her strong, looking her in the eye. "I was *infatuated*, yes, but when she chose Hammond and I saw her true character for the first time, I was not only repulsed by her, but by what I had let myself fall for. I went to Italy to clear my head, but I did not need the space to heal from her. That happened before."

"But when you came to take leave of my father, I watched you. I saw the longing in your eyes as you spoke to Rose."

Adam shook his head. "There was no longing. Only disgust. How the mind can perceive things so faulty at times."

Cori considered his words. It made sense, of course. But it was not easy to wrap her head around. The letters Rosemary had clandestinely sent him painted a romantic picture of young love and a promised future. A future he now claims he had let go of before even leaving England.

"And as far as hiding away," he said, "I have been unable to write any of my correspondence these past few weeks because my new wife has had me thoroughly distracted."

Cori glanced up sharply. "How do you mean?"

"I mean," he placed a light kiss on her forehead, "that I've been too busy thinking of you to get much of anything done. That is why I must constantly go to my study to take care of business. There is no business being taken care of."

Cori grinned as Adam kissed her cheek. "Perhaps I have misunderstood."

"It seems to me you've misunderstood a wealth of things," he murmured before taking her lips once again.

Later when they mounted their horses, Adam said, "I am sorry that I was not more honest about my relationship with Rosemary. It was thoughtless of me. I should have considered that you would wonder about it."

Cori nodded, pulling Chance up beside Adam's horse. "I admit I was confused to learn that you proposed to her first."

His head jerked up. "I never proposed to your sister."

The women's voices repeated in her mind. "I heard it at the wedding breakfast."

Shaking his head, he regarded her closely. "I do not know what gossip you heard, but I have never asked Rosemary to be my wife."

Calm spread through her, and her joy grew when he asked, "Will you dance with me this evening at Lady Dunview's ball?"

"Yes, of course."

He cleared his throat. "I've also got some news."

Cori watched him expectantly. His face distorted in an expression of apology.

"My family has returned from London, and our mothers have come up with a plan." He ran a hand through his hair, then directed his horse toward home. "It seems Rosemary has become fodder for excessive gossip. She is having trouble finding a suitor in Town, and your mother fears she has lost hope of a respectable match."

"Because of Lord Hammond's death?" That did not add up.

He shook his head. "No, she has developed a reputation of being loose. She was found alone with a man, embracing. Her character has been called into question. Your mother has approached mine, and they believe if we lend her our consequence, she can overcome the scandal before it blows out of proportion. She might regain some respectability if we are to chaperone her."

A pit formed in her gut, growing heavy with increasing dread. Was it normal to care very little for one's sister's lost respectability? Cori did not wish Rosemary ill, but chaperoning her about society was a sure way to lose the little footing she had just attained with her husband. They were only beginning to know one another.

Training her gaze straight ahead, she asked, "Do you wish to chaperone her?"

"No."

Her breath caught, his answer so sure and swift. She looked over sharply, his sincere, deliberate face bouncing with the horse's gait.

"I do not find her conducive to our developing relationship," he continued.

Temptation to ask him about the letters hidden within his desk flitted to the surface, but Cori shoved them back down. He had already stated he did not love Rosemary, he had quit his attraction when her character was made plain to him. And he had not proposed. That was enough, wasn't it?

"Then we are decided," she said. "We will refuse to help."

CHAPTER 16

$\mathcal{T}$he house and courtyard was a flurry of servants when they arrived back at the barn. People moved this way and that carrying trunks and boxes, putting away horses and cleaning the mud encrusted carriage.

"Prepare yourself," Adam muttered, worried about Cori. She had reached a new place with him, and now she had to reside in the house with his mother. He groaned.

"What is it?" his wife asked, concern on her pretty brow.

"Nothing frightening," he smiled back. "But let us be clear on one thing. Regardless of any emotional blackmail, we will stand firm together."

They crossed the lawn and entered the foyer to hear Lady Berwind shouting orders at various servants. No wonder everyone adored Cori; she was significantly less abrasive.

"Adam! You've returned," Mother said, approaching him with her cheek out, which he dutifully kissed.

"And Corianne," she said, giving Cori her hands.

"My name is Coriander, but you may call me Cori. Most people do."

Mother blinked, her face a picture of condescension. She

turned to the passing chambermaid and requested a bath to be prepared in her room forthwith. "I must rest," she explained to the couple.

"We have been invited to Lady Dunview's ball this evening," Adam said.

"Splendid," Mother replied.

"Did Travis return with you?" he asked.

"No, he chose to stay in Town."

"And Father?"

Her eyes tightened. "In bed. The trip was rough and he needs to recover. He was seen by a wonderful physician and has a new regimen in place. I am sure we can fill you in on it if you wish."

Adam nodded.

"Until tonight," she said, mounting the stairs.

Adam swallowed his irritation. If Travis was ever going to create a real profession for himself then he needed to begin taking things seriously. And if his father was going to teach him all he needed to know to take over as the marquess, he needed to heal.

"I believe I am going to bathe as well," Cori said quietly, pulling him from his brooding thoughts.

He smiled, watching her go and wondering where in his life he went right to have such an amazing woman by his side.

ADAM FELT the air shift while he descended the stairs. He reached the foyer and stilled, the sight of Rosemary awaiting him a gross opposite of the angel he had anticipated: his wife.

"May I help you?" he asked stiffly, avoiding any close proximity to the blonde vixen.

Her lips curled in a way he used to admire; now, however, her smile only disgusted him further. "I believe your mother has informed you that I require an escort? How kind of you to take on the role." She stepped up beside him, her fingers trailing lightly down his arm.

A small noise behind them turned his chest cold and he spun, cringing at Cori's crestfallen face. He moved to her side but she was stone, her arm unyielding when he tried to thread it through his own.

"Rosemary, how lovely to see you," Mother said, coming down the stairs with regal authority, her vivid maroon gown the height of fashion. "Let us be off."

They rode to the ball in silence. Appreciating the darkness as a cover, Adam picked up Cori's hand in his own and held it quietly on the seat, his mother and Rosemary across from him completely unaware. She slipped her dainty hand from his grip. Anger flared within him at her careless sister—for there could be no other cause for Cori's sudden distance. Drat Rosemary!

"It shall be lovely to see all of our country friends again." Mother sighed. "We can tell them all about London."

A floral scent wafted from Cori's hair and Adam inhaled, trying to place the flower. It was not roses, of that he was certain. And neither was it lavender.

"It shall be splendid going to parties again," Rosemary said, causing Cori to stiffen beside him. "How amusing to remind us of the many joyful entertainments we once shared."

The carriage rolled to a stop, and Adam's mouth remained closed. He did not know how to reply, for the woman was cunning and would likely twist any of his words. It was evident she intended to hurt her sister, but to what aim was lost on him.

CORI DID NOT KNOW whether to run and cry, or stay and swallow her feelings. Rosemary's game was anyone's guess, and her words were hurtful. She could not look at her sister without recalling the loving notes she had sent Adam so long ago, and resulting anger and frustration warred within her. Coming down the stairs to the image of Rosemary and Adam in a close *tête-à-tête* was all of her recent fears realized, and she had to remind herself that Adam did not care for her sister in that way.

She needed to trust her husband.

They walked into the ballroom, Cori's hands firmly hidden within the folds of her gown. Her gaze flitted from face to interested face and she swallowed, unused to the direct attention the party was heaping on her. It seemed everyone wanted a glimpse of the earl's new wife.

The strains of a waltz began and Adam turned, grasping her elbow; his deliberate gaze trained on her own. "Please excuse us, I should like to dance with my wife."

He whisked her onto the center of the dance floor, his arm coming around her waist, supporting her, his other grasping her hand. The strength of his gaze was enough to make her cower, but she stood strong.

"She was merely greeting me. I did not approach her."

Cori laughed. *Of course* Rosemary was to blame. That was not up for debate.

Adam stopped in the center of the dance floor. "Can you not simply trust me?"

She did trust him. It was her sister that angered her.

Yet, Cori could not help but think of the letters, of his previous attachment. She realized that he did not love Rosemary. But if he did not marry her to spite Rosemary, then why *did* he marry her? She had believed him when he explained his feelings for Rosemary and their subsequent demise, but watching her sister standing so close to his side, her stomach had dropped and all sense failed her.

Grasping her hand he swiftly fled the ballroom, pulling her down the hall and onto an open terrace. "Must we rehash this now?"

Cori glared, anger coursing through her. "It was not I caught in an embrace this evening, Adam. And I did not choose to allow Rosemary to accompany us. I thought we decided to deny our mothers' request."

"I was set upon!" he defended. "I did not anticipate her presence, she was merely there. What do you propose I should have done?"

Cori watched him, her heart constricting with sorrow. She wanted so badly to put her trust in him but fear reared its ugly head and she quaked with apprehension.

"I've read the letters," she said, surprising herself.

Confusion marred his brow.

"From Rosemary. In your desk."

Comprehension lit Adam's face. "Those were from years ago," he explained. "Before she had ever set foot in London. Before she even met Lord Hammond or her numerous other suitors."

"Yes, and you've kept them close all these years," Cori said, fighting the emotion rising to the surface. "I read the words she wrote, the way she talked of your future together. It was made clear to me that I was a pawn in your game. I understand you chose me to spite her, and I find it is a difficult thing to come to terms with."

Adam stood still, his mouth slack as he searched her face. She waited for him to speak, for a denial to spill from his lips, but nothing was forthcoming.

Wiping tears from her cheeks with the back of her hand, Cori turned and walked calmly from the terrace. She regained her composure as best she could and reentered the ballroom, accepting a dance from a neighbor and doing her utmost to appear calm and collected.

She would be able to vent her emotions into her pillow at the evenings end. For now, she simply had to endure.

IF IT WOULDN'T SEND him directly to Newgate Prison, Adam would gleefully wring her neck. He watched Rosemary across the dance floor, anger coursing through him. He wanted, desperately, to drag her from the dance floor and put her in her place. But causing a scene would not benefit any member of his family. He cared little for his own reputation, but deeply for Cori's. For her, he would refrain.

"Cards, old boy?"

He turned sharply, smiling at the older man to his left. Lord Fordham, an old crony of his father's, appeared as bored as he sounded.

Lord Fordham continued, "I find these balls dashedly dull. Dance a few times and get out of here, that's my advice."

Nodding, Adam searched the room for Cori. She was dancing the cotillion and looked radiant doing it. Her smile, he noticed, was tight. Her mouth closed to conversation. He wanted nothing more than to erase her troubles, and he vowed to do so.

It was foolish of him to have remained quiet earlier, when she had first accused him of his spiteful motives. In truth, it was the first he had considered the concept and he was too busy examining the idea to properly shut it down.

"How's your father these days?" Lord Fordham said, causing him to jump.

"Unwell. But he has been in London seeing doctors and we are hopeful."

"Capital. Excellent man, your father."

Adam looked at the older man. He'd lost his wife a few years before. "Why do you attend these balls, sir? You lack the females to drag you here."

Lord Fordham smiled softly, his white side whiskers quivering. Reminiscing, perhaps? "I must, boy. Someday you'll understand."

Adam watched him go. He approached a young woman and then led her onto the floor. For an older man, he was spry.

He chuckled to himself. He would likely never understand the older earl.

Checking the floor once again for Cori, he watched her leave one partner and join another for a Scottish reel. Rosemary now danced with Lord Fordham, and his mother stood just on the other side of the room deep in conversation with a few women.

If he was not going to dance with his wife, then he was not going to dance at all. He might as well take Lord Fordham's advice and go play some cards.

CHAPTER 17

*C*ori refused the dance with the older lord whose name she failed to recall. His wiry white side whiskers quivered as he smiled, bowing himself away.

Taking the opportunity for respite, she sat in a chair along the wall, watching silk skirts twirl around the floor and trussed up gentlemen lead the ladies from one step to the next. The quadrille was a stately dance and she was only too happy to give her aching feet a rest.

"I haven't seen Adam in some time," Rosemary said, sidling up and taking the empty seat beside her.

Cori stiffened. The familiar use of her husband's name was likely geared toward her discomfort. And it worked.

"When we used to attend the balls years ago, he would scarce leave my side." She sighed. "I vow, he was the most dedicated gentleman of the lot."

"The lot?" Cori asked. "Are you referring to the many men you strung along?"

Rosemary's smile slipped momentarily.

Turning to face her sister, Cori asked, "And where are they now, Rose?"

Silence met her question, but Cori did not back down. There was nothing to gain from Rosemary's words or actions. She could not have Adam, now or ever, and her spiteful reminiscing helped no one.

"Rosemary, can you not let it go?"

"No," she said, her voice as hard as her face. "I had a perfect plan, and you ruined everything."

"I am sorry you feel that way, but what good are your actions going to do now? How is it helpful to sabotage my marriage?"

"It will make me feel better," she said.

Cori's heart broke, her fears realized. Rosemary had no plan in mind, no ulterior motive. She simply wished Cori and Adam ill will.

Standing, she looked down at her older, more beautiful sister. "I am sorry you are struggling. I know I needn't remind you that these trials are of your own making, for mere recollection can tell you so. But I will say one thing on the matter and then never speak of it again: you will not ruin my marriage, regardless of your efforts. I love my husband. Which is more than I can say for how he ever felt about you. You had your chance with him and I am glad to say you lost it. Move on, Rose."

"That is the prettiest speech I have ever heard."

Cori gasped, turning to find Adam standing directly behind her. "And," he continued, taking her hands in his own, "those letters meant nothing to me. In truth, I forgot they were there or I would have burned them long ago. Cori, I did not marry you to spite Rosemary, I married you because you are thoughtful, intelligent and kind. You serve others without thought of yourself, you care about people, and you have a stunning heart. I am blessed I did not fall for any other traps, so I was prepared to offer for you when I finally met you."

"But you said nothing when I made the accusation."

Adam pulled her a few paces away from Rosemary, allowing

for some privacy. She noticed her sister stalk away and felt the relief her departure brought.

"I should have, but I was too busy pondering your words. Until that moment I had not even considered the possibility. In truth, I wondered if Rosemary *was* part of my motive. Upon recollection, though, I do not think it ever crossed my mind, as a subconscious motive or otherwise. I was smitten with you, Cori. You attracted me from the beginning."

She shook her head. His words were lovely, but could they be true?

He stepped closer. "I may not have loved you the moment I asked you to marry me, but the more fool me. I love you now, Cori Arnett, and my love shall only grow stronger with time. Allow me to prove it to you every day, and you will know with a surety that you are the one. The only one."

Heart soaring, Cori stepped marginally closer. "Very well, Adam. But you could have told me sooner."

He leaned down and kissed her, his face spreading into a grin when he stepped away. "I have a novel idea."

"Hmm?" she asked, wrapped in the glow from his kiss like a warm blanket.

"I believe we are a due a wedding trip. Where shall we go?"

"Italy? I should like a tour from someone who knows the place well."

He grinned. "Italy it is. On one condition."

"Yes?"

"Tell me what you smell of. I have been dying to know for weeks."

She smiled softly. "Jessamine."

EPILOGUE

ori stood on the bow of the deck, the salty wind whipping strands of hair into her face. She smoothed them away, soaking in the Italian coastline peeking through the distance. Warm arms wrapped around her, pulling her against a solid chest. She leaned her head back, allowing Adam's warmth to seep through her gown and heat her skin.

"I cannot wait to show you the Roman ruins," he said. "And the food, Cori, is absolutely amazing."

"I suppose I ought to eat a great deal more, if I am going to be supporting another human."

She felt him stiffen behind her.

"You cannot mean it?" he asked softly. His hands trailed up her arms, gripping her shoulders to turn her around. His eyes grew wide, his mouth hung slack.

Cori nodded. "Mr. Gallo confirmed it this morning."

His face breaking into a grin, Adam swept her into his arms, spinning her in circles as he whooped. Setting her down in a sudden, rapid movement his hands steadied her. "Are you alright? I should not have done that."

She chuckled. "A little queasy, perhaps. But no worse for the wear."

Pulling her into a soft embrace, Adam's arms held her securely. He kissed the top of her head. "We shall grow this child on Italian food and then take him back to England to be born among his countrymen."

Pulling back, she lifted an eyebrow. "What has you so convinced it is to be a boy?"

"I need an heir," he said simply.

She shook her head. "You cannot control these things, Adam. What if she is a little girl?" Despite the fellow passenger and physician, Dr. Gallo's, healthy examination, a dose of concern for her unborn child remained at the forefront of her thoughts. She needed to know the child would be loved regardless of her inability to inherit Adam's title.

"I will love her almost as much as I love her mother," he said solemnly. "And I have a strong feeling she will have me wrapped around her finger just as much."

Grinning, Cori reached up on tip toe to kiss her husband. "Of course she will. She'll learn from the best."

SNEAK PEEK AT THE JEWELS OF HALSTEAD MANOR

CHAPTER ONE

*G*iulia stood in the center of the lane and watched the carriage bound away down the pocked road, jarring the passengers seated on top of the swaying conveyance. She had only just been among those who couldn't afford passage inside the stagecoach, and cringed watching Mr. Bradley, the older gentleman she'd sat beside earlier, clutching his seat to remain upright on the careening vehicle.

Cold autumn air rushed into her lungs as Mr. Bradley nearly toppled off the roof. She squeezed her hands together as if maintaining a rigid posture would keep the elderly gentleman atop the carriage and waited for what felt like ages. Mr. Bradley righted himself, lifting one hand in a tentative wave and she eagerly responded, trying—and failing—to ignore the pity she could detect in his kind, old eyes.

The conveyance turned out of view and Giulia spun in a full circle slowly taking in the vast expanse of empty land that seemed to continue in every direction without end. The sun brushed the edge of the sky, already dipping behind the horizon. Looming darkness nipped at her heels and she picked up the rope Ames had tied to her trunk. Gripping her valise over her shoulder, she pivoted away from the declining sun and walked in the opposite direction.

According to the stage driver, this road would end at Halstead Manor. The long, empty lane looked daunting, and Giulia's stomach complained as she began her trek. Or, rather, continued the rather long and tedious journey that had begun eight months prior when her father took his final breath on Africa's soil. Or any soil, for that matter. It was not entirely possible to take a breath anywhere when one was dead.

Giulia moved as briskly as her trunk would allow and tried not to watch the distance for buildings, gates, or obvious signs that she was nearing her uncle's home. That would only make the walk longer.

Uncle Robert. The *elusive* Uncle Robert. How had she come to be in a position where the only person she could turn to was the man who was single-handedly responsible for keeping her own father from his childhood home? She swallowed the apprehension that bubbled up into her throat and shook her head.

Uncle Robert had written to her. She had proof. He had invited her to come. She dropped the rope tethered to her trunk and opened her valise, feeling the folded missive tucked into the pocket and absorbing the calming balm of hope. She would not be turned away, she reminded herself. She was invited.

The sun continued its descent and Giulia felt the lack of warmth on her back as it fell behind her. She trudged down the lane, pulling her trunk and readjusting the valise on her shoulder. The luggage was heavy and beginning to slow her down. She was tempted to hide it away on the side of the road, but there was no bush or ditch sufficient to lend coverage. Sighing, she pulled harder. What else could she do? In it was every earthly possession she owned.

Ames had seen to that.

A smile tugged at her lips at the memory. His dark hair falling over his brow and the half-smile that tilted his mouth up.

The footman-turned-valet-turned-man-of-all-work had been in Giulia's life since before she could remember. As her lifestyle had altered, his job had altered with it. He was eight years her senior, but that had never stopped her from fantasizing over a future shared with the man. She hardly cared if marriage to Ames would lower her alleged station in life, for she had lived like a servant for half of it anyway. At least, she had done so after her mother left.

Giulia pushed thoughts of Ames from her mind. Dwelling on the man would do her no good, at present. He was in London starting his business, and she would make do with clandestine letters until they could be reunited again.

She had devised a plan. Ames would address his letters to her father, which would naturally be passed on to her. It was foolproof. No one need know she was corresponding with a man whom she was not yet engaged to and Ames's notes would fall in with the rest of them easily enough. Letters addressed to her father were bound to pour into Halstead Manor since she had given her new direction to her father's publisher. Adventurers of the world seemed unlikely to give up on Patrick Pepper and his assistant, Jules, anytime soon.

Giulia's foot collided with an object and she pitched forward, sprawling on the rough dirt road. Pushing up onto her knees, she looked behind her to find a heap lying prostrate in the lane. Shadows fell behind the dark figure, blending it into the road.

The heap shifted slightly, and a low groan emanated from one end—the end which had snagged her foot. It was a person.

No, it was a *man*.

Giulia quietly got to her feet and rounded the edge of the crumpled form toward her discarded luggage. He groaned once more, causing her to jump. Shaking herself, Giulia focused. Father had taught her to be cautious, but he had also taught her to be kind. And this man was clearly hurt. Squaring her shoulders, Giulia straightened her spine and looked in unabashed courage toward the fallen man.

"Sir?"

Nothing.

She stepped closer and bent slightly, hoping to ascertain the man's status from his clothing. The near darkness made that an impossible feat. But what sort of man would find himself in this position? Could he be a ruffian? Or perhaps a drunken workman fallen on his way home from the pub? Giulia glanced around her again. Unlikely. There was no building in sight, let alone a pub. And according to the stage driver, this lane led to one place, and one place only. Halstead Manor.

Giulia bent lower and raised her voice slightly. "Sir? Are you alert?"

A mumble came from the man. It was as easy to discern as his clothing in the fading light. So, not at all.

She stood, hesitating. It was growing far too dark to see what she was dealing with.

A hand shot out and grabbed her ankle before she could move away. A heart wrenching cry escaped the man and his grip immediately slackened.

Worry moved into Giulia's gut and churned. The sudden and inappropriate feeling of the man's hand on her ankle was instantly overshadowed by the pain in his voice. This was no drunken farmer; he was hurt.

Giulia dropped to her knees and did not hesitate as her nursing instincts kicked in. She felt up and down each arm before moving to his neck. He lay face down, his head bent away from her. Her eyes were adjusted to the dim lighting and she took notice of his clothing. Even if the dark made it utterly impossible to see, she would have known who he was by the feel of the fine wool that made his coat. The high-quality neck-cloth circling his throat. The polished shine of his hessians caught out of the corner of her eye.

This man was a gentleman.

His neck and head fully examined, Giulia moved lower, feeling along his broad shoulders. Part of her hoped not to find injury, but she knew it was a fruitless wish and waited in anticipation for the recoil that would show her exactly where he hurt. Hopefully before she had to move much lower.

Her fingers kneaded the muscle of his far shoulder and worked their way inward. She reached the shoulder blade closest to herself and he cried out again, a split second before her fingertips landed in something wet.

Wet, warm, and gooey.

Blood.

Oh, heavens. It was a blessed thing she wasn't the fainting type.

After feeling a little further, she dug her hand under the man's body and felt the underside of the wound. Well, that was a relief. It had to be a bullet and it must have gone clean through.

Shifting to access the bottom of her petticoats, Giulia ripped off a length of fabric and turned back to the patient. How was she to wrap him if she could not get him into a sitting position?

"Sir, are you alert? What is your name?"

He mumbled, but the sound was incoherent.

Giulia did her best to focus her gaze. "I need to wrap your shoulder and it would ease my job immensely if I could get you to sit up. Or lean, perhaps. Do you think, sir, that you might be able to lean?"

A muffled groan sounded in the darkness. Giulia tried to take a calming breath and crawled to the opposite side of her patient before leaning down to get close to his face. Groaning was a good sign usually; it showed a level of consciousness. Now she only needed to determine just how conscious he was.

She placed a finger beneath his nose and felt his breath. It was coming in short, rapid spurts, but she already knew that by the quick rise and fall of his back. She could see enough of his face to determine that it was pinched, and sent a prayer up asking for guidance. How was she going to help a nearly incoherent stranger when she was stuck in the middle of nowhere, no buildings for miles?

She brought her face nearly level with the patient's, her body contorted so that she could look him in the eyes without actually lying down in the dirt.

"Please open your eyes," she murmured calmly. "I need to be sure you are awake so I may talk you through my treatment plan." What she truly needed was to assure herself that the man would remain alive long enough for her to fetch help, but she would keep that to herself.

His eyelids fluttered slightly before peeking open.

Success!

Then they closed. She frowned.

"I would like to turn you over and lay you against my valise. We need to elevate your torso to slow the bleeding. And it will make my job of wrapping you a tad easier." She waited a moment and watched his lashes flutter. He grimaced deeper, if that was possible, and opened his eyes again with what appeared to be determination.

Giulia grinned. That was a welcome trait for a man in his position. She retrieved her bag in haste, returning to his side. "Do not strain, sir. I do not wish to cause further stress to your injury."

She positioned her valise near the man's good shoulder.

Giulia took a breath. "When I count to three I am going to roll you onto the bag. Ready?"

She slid her hands under the man's chest and wished, not for the first time, that Ames was with her. His strength would have made this an easy task. Harnessing power from the inner confidence that this was a necessary action to save the man's life, and the simple truth that she had no other option than to attempt it alone, Giulia took a sustaining breath.

"One. Two. *Three!*" She grunted on the last count and heaved with every bit of strength her body possessed. To her astonishment, he rolled easily. Whether by sheer will or the unlikely possibility that he may have helped, the injured man was turned over and propped up on her valise, making his shoulder accessible and elevated.

Perfect.

"Splendid," Giulia said cheerfully as she clapped her hands together and sat back on her heels. "Now, don't you go anywhere. I am going to fetch my sewing shears and then we will have this coat off of you in a jiffy."

He grunted, seemingly in response, and she moved to her trunk to retrieve her scissors. Father often said her excessive talking was a virtue and not a failing, but she sometimes wondered if it would be better for her mouth to remain closed. This man seemed somewhat lucid; just *how* lucid, she could not determine. If she could do anything to distract him from her poking and prodding, it was worth trying.

"I suppose I ought to introduce myself, given this extraordinary circumstance. I am Giulia." She sighed. "I wish I knew your name. That would make our situation less awkward, do you not agree? Perhaps I should give you one." She slid the scissors between the man's neck and her valise, using her fingers to guide them, and began carefully snipping the coat away. She was used to assisting the doctor in the dim light of a ship's cabin as it rolled upon the waves, but even then she'd had at least one candle to light the room.

"Just a nickname, of course," she continued, then wrinkled her brow. "Though I cannot see your face clearly, so that adds a level of difficulty to the act of naming you. I must come up with something, however." She hummed for a moment while she thought and continued to snip away the fine coat. "This is certainly a shame, is it not? What a fine coat to utterly ruin in such a barbaric manner. Though, to be fair, the large hole in the shoulder rendered it ruined long before I came at you with my sewing shears."

Giulia clucked her tongue. The wound was substantial, from what she could tell. She only hoped she was successfully distracting him. "I've got it! I will call you Trouble! That is what we are in, don't you agree?"

He groaned and she ceased cutting. "You do not like Trouble? No, you are right. It does not roll off the tongue so easily, does it?" Giulia looked up as clouds began to move away from the moon on the horizon, lighting the scene around her and giving her a better view of her patient. "Glorious. We must thank the moon. How kind of her to come out right when I could use her light. Now, where were we?" She resumed cutting and noticed the grimace back on the man's face. It was easier to decipher now, though not by much. The blood that dripped from his wound gleamed in the moonlight and hastened her work.

"Right, we were naming you. Hmmm, I think...yes! I've got it! *Danger.* I shall call you Danger. It is fitting, don't you agree? You clearly are in some yourself, though how that came to be is not hardly fathomable to me, given our location. And has your horse run off, Danger, or were you walking along this lane alone?" She unbuttoned the front of the coat and pulled off the portion she had cut off, talking while gently removing the clothing. Then she moved on to the waistcoat, working as quickly as her chilled fingers allowed her to. The man's injury was alarming enough, but in the back of her mind, Giulia couldn't stop thinking about *who* caused the injury in the first place; she had no guarantee the aggressor wasn't still a threat. She would not be comfortable until they were removed indoors somewhere, safe.

Nerves loosened her tongue further. "I suppose I cannot say it is totally unreasonable to go without a horse, since I was walking along the lane alone myself. But I cannot say it is *normal* behavior, for it certainly is not normal for me."

Giulia made quick work of the waistcoat, removing it from the injured shoulder while leaving what she could on the rest of the man to warm him. His loss of blood was evident in the pallor of his skin and she did her best to distract him with her chatter while no doubt adding to his pain. Once she got to his shirt, she removed his cravat and set it aside while cutting a hole in the shirt for access. Whoever this gentleman was, he clearly maintained activity that built his physique, for Giulia had done her fair share of nurse work on other men, and few had come near this man's breadth or firm display of muscle. Had he not worn the clothing of a gentleman, she would have assumed him to be a laborer.

She threw the inappropriate thoughts from her mind. How could she examine a man's physique so thoroughly? What would Ames think if he knew how she was admiring this complete and total stranger? Her vicinity to the man and the intimacy involved in her care of his wound was questionable enough. Now that she was back in England, she would have to take care, to act the part of a lady—as Father had asked of her.

She mentally shook herself and returned her attention to Danger with a smile on her face. Not that it mattered, for his eyes were screwed shut. But she liked to think the smile could be heard through her voice.

"I do wish I had some laudanum to give you. It would put you to sleep though, and then I would be forced to talk to myself. That is not quite an attractive idea, I feel." She wadded up his cravat and pressed it against the wound on the front of the shoulder where the majority of the blood was pooling before picking up the strips of ripped petticoat and using them to wrap underneath his arm and around his neck to firmly hold the cravat in place.

"Danger, you must not think me selfish." Giulia tied off the bandage and then dropped a hand to his and squeezed his fingers in a show of support. He did not squeeze back, his cold, calloused hand still beneath her touch. She swallowed. "I do promise that if I had laudanum at my disposal, I would not hesitate to administer it to you. It would be much more pleasant to talk to myself than to sit here and know that I am causing you pain. Please keep in mind though, that what I am doing will undoubtedly help you feel better eventually, for I have staunched the bleeding. You must feel more secure with this wrap in place, yes? Now, for the chill."

She released his hand and moved to her trunk before pulling out her winter pelisse, a nice, fur-lined garment of blue wool. "This should do the trick," Giulia murmured as she laid the pelisse over the large man, covering his torso and legs down to his knees. She stared below his knees for a moment, her brow furrowing.

"I am afraid I have nothing to cover your legs. Nor any food to give you for sustenance." Her stomach growled on cue. "I promise that was not to prove my innocence," she said with a smile and tucked the pelisse around Danger's shoulders and waist. "Now, I am trying to determine if it would be foolish to continue on this road, or if I should go back the way I came and attempt to flag down any passing carriages. I do think that given the late hour, I may have more luck if I continue onward. My father always said I was a quick runner, though that is entirely unladylike so you must promise never to reveal that tidbit of information. I have only shared it with you now, Danger, so that you will not be alarmed at my choice to leave you. I cannot possibly sit around here and wait on this deserted road for help. And that is no exaggeration; it truly does seem quite deserted."

She wondered briefly if it would be safe to leave him alone. He'd found some reason to get himself shot in the first place. Could Danger's foe return to finish the job? Unlikely. Given the blood loss and incoherence of her patient, it had been some time since the wound had been inflicted. The assailant was surely long gone. She *hoped*. No, if there was any danger in leaving Danger, it was only the possibility of a carriage coming this way and not seeing him.

Giulia chewed on her lip and looked at the strained expression on the stranger's face. He did not have much time. He needed a doctor right away.

She shot to her feet. "I will be quick, Danger. I am leaving all of my possessions with you, so you must guard them. I am trusting you with everything I own."

Danger's lip twitched and Giulia stifled a gasp. It could have been a trick of the moonlight, but it looked as if he was fighting a smile. That was a very good sign and her heart soared. She took off in the direction of Halstead Manor and ran with all of her might.

ABOUT THE AUTHOR

Kasey Stockton is a staunch lover of all things romantic. She doesn't discriminate between genres and enjoys a wide variety of happily ever afters. Drawn to the Regency period at a young age when gifted a copy of *Sense and Sensibility* by her grandmother, Kasey initially began writing Regency romances. She has since written in a variety of genres, but all of her titles fall under sweet romance. A native of northern California, she now resides in Texas with her own prince charming and their three children. When not reading, writing, or binge-watching chick flicks, she enjoys running, cutting hair, and anything chocolate.

Made in the USA
Columbia, SC
15 January 2022

53834194R00079